LITERARY LARCENY

A SHELF INDULGENCE COZY MYSTERY

S.E. BABIN

Cover art by Lou Harper from Cover Affairs

Published by Oliver-Heber Books

0 9 8 7 6 5 4 3 2 1

ONE

Having a book in my hand turned even the worst day around. I lounged on my couch with Poppy curled up beside me, reading the latest murder mystery from one of my favorite up-and-coming authors. Her writing had incredible voice—humor, snark, spine-tingling crime. It was everything I ever wanted in a thriller.

Idly, I stroked Poppy's silky orange fur, her satisfied purr making me chuckle. She rarely cuddled up to me like this. We had a good relationship, but Poppy wasn't the most affectionate of cats. For the longest time, I thought she barely tolerated me. After all, I purchased the bookstore with her in it. I'd hold a grudge over that, too.

But Poppy had come a long way, and over the time we'd spent together, I realized she had a sharp intellect for a domesticated animal, and an odd knack for sniffing out murderers. Not that I wanted my pet to have a gift like that, but since murder had come knocking on my door too many times for comfort, I had to appreciate it.

This snuggling, though?

This was brand new.

I suspect it had come because Poppy sensed I was nursing a broken heart. Some people might say animals don't possess the capacity for empathy. I thought that was a bunch of hogwash. Poppy had stayed plastered to my side the moment my heart had broken and hadn't left it since. We'd taken a new step in our sometimes-odd relationship, and I was more grateful than ever for her.

Hardy and I were broken up and had been ever since his ex-fiancée had wandered back into his life with a blue-eyed, dark-haired little girl. I had no doubt she belonged to him, and I would never stand in the way of him forming a relationship with her or the child's mother, Hardy's apparent ex-fiancée. The thought sent grief spearing through my heart.

Every time I thought I was over the sharp sting of this, it hit me right in the face when I least expected it.

Only time would make it better.

Distance, too. I couldn't control time, but I could control where I went and at what time. Hardy was some-what predictable. His work hours stayed the same, and he liked to eat lunch at the same few places every day. I'd done my best to avoid those places, and so far, I had yet to catch a glimpse of him.

But it wasn't all bad. Instead of paying off my mort-gage, I purchased the adjoining building where Sprinkle

Heaven used to be. The construction crew had been there for two weeks now, expanding part of the bookstore, and building out a new venture I was still nervous about.

The idea of a private investigation firm was a seed I'd nurtured for a while now, but since I was with Hardy at the time, I shelved it. He would hate it, and I had loved him more than I wanted to be a PI. Even now, with the new place all planned out, down to the specific type of rug on the grey, ceramic floor, I had reservations.

I loved books and had no intention of giving up my store, but like Poppy, I seemed to have a knack with solving murders and the occasional other type of crime. Tattered Pages, my store, was running smooth as butter, so I could afford to step away to start up a new venture. Harper, my assistant, was invaluable to both me and my store. I paid her generously for her efforts, and she was ecstatic to take over more of the day-to-day operations of the store.

Daniel Jensen, a good friend and chess cheater, had encouraged this venture and suggested I call the place Turning the Page. I hated that I liked it. He'd be smug about it for months. Sighing, I slid a bookmark between pages and put the book down on the coffee table. Poppy shifted next to me, her purr a soft rumble against my side.

The sun was close to setting, stripes of purple and red streaking through the evening sky. I was back in my house now. After the break-in, I'd stayed with Hardy for a while. Until...everything. I'd moved out right away but chose to stay in a local bed-and-breakfast until I could get someone over to change out the doors for something sturdier. I also changed out all the windows from regular to security glass. None of the changes were 100 percent foolproof, but someone would need to be very determined to get inside.

I had no issues once I solved the last case, and the new security measures made me feel safer.

Things were different, but different wasn't bad.

Change could be good. It encouraged growth, and I had to admit, after everything, I felt a lot better about the future than I did before. Not that everything was rosy right now, but I had a clean slate.

The world was my oyster.

I just had to get my hands dirty and shuck it.

I WOKE up bright and early the next morning. Tattered Pages was closed on weekends now, and I had a list made up of things I needed to take care of. Poppy opened one bright eye when I turned on the lamp, blinked, then buried her head underneath her blanket.

I laughed and slid out of bed, hoping I remembered to program the coffee pot.

As soon as I stepped into the hall, the scent of fresh coffee swirled through the air. Relieved I'd remembered to program it, I padded straight to the kitchen, snagged the mug next to the machine and poured myself a cup.

The sun wasn't up, and everything was quiet. Birds weren't yet chirping outside, traffic was at a bare minimum, and the only sound was the soft rumble of the coffee pot. I could sit here and ponder things in silence, just me and my thoughts.

Normally when I got up, Poppy followed me to the kitchen, but she chose to stay in the bedroom this morning, so I shrugged on a cardigan and carried my coffee outside. A few weeks ago, I'd put new comfy chairs outside on the porch. I curled up in one of them and settled in to watch the sun come up.

The temperatures had cooled significantly over the last few weeks, the morning air a bracing bite that had me tugging my sweater closer. Steam curled over the mug, teasing my nose. I inhaled and smiled, feeling relaxed for the first time in a while.

I lived in a beautiful area, especially during the summertime. Winter got a little wild, but I'd rather have mild summers and deal with worse winters than brutal summers like those poor people in the South dealt with. But it was times like these, when the fresh air ruffled my hair and the scent of pine teased my nose, that all felt right with the world.

Even when the world was falling down around my ears.

I looked at my To-Do list and tried not to get overwhelmed.

A colleague of mine from Copper Canyon, a neighboring town, sent me an email a few days ago asking for my help with something. She wouldn't tell me what it was but insisted I come as soon as possible.

Georgia wasn't the kind of person who made demands

or exaggerated about things, so I didn't take offense to her request. I emailed her back and told her I'd be over on Saturday—today.

We'd met a few weeks back when we did a neighboring county book sale. Silverwood Hollow, Candlelight Springs, Copper Canyon, and Martindale booksellers had gathered in our town square and put on a massive sale, bringing tourists in from all over the state. I had plenty of books I needed to let go of. From the aggressive dog-eared books handled by customers who never planned to buy anything in the first place, to returns, and shipping damage, Tattered Pages led the pack with the offerings.

Harriet Tulle from Binders had brought over almost as many, but Georgia only brought a few boxes and seemed completely blindsided when she saw how much we had. We had a good laugh about it and ended up striking up a friendly relationship. I wouldn't call her a friend yet, but it seemed headed that way.

Over the last few weeks, we'd exchanged almost daily emails, but this one had an urgent note from her I'd never heard before. She was first on my list today. Then I had to check on construction for the bookstore expansion and hit the grocery store before I got home. My fridge was in a sorry state, and Daniel would be over later to beat me at chess.

A smile tilted my lips. Daniel was a good guy, even if he was an unapologetic cheater when it came to games. I couldn't figure out how he was doing it, though, so I couldn't stop him. Instead, I brushed up on strategies and gave him a run for his money despite his cheating. I also rarely left the table now, even if my bladder was screaming.

Consequently, I won more games than ever now, much to his consternation.

He knew about Hardy and hadn't said much, perhaps sensing I needed stability rather than judgment—for Hardy or for me. He'd done that, giving me a solid shoulder to lean on without forcing me to talk about things. Daniel listened when I tried to talk about it, occasionally throwing out nuggets of advice, but he never once brought things up when I hadn't.

There weren't many men who could listen without trying to fix things, and it made me value our friendship more than ever. Plus, Daniel was a great guinea pig when it came to trying out all the new recipes I had saved in my bookmarks. Tonight's offering was a twist on Bolognese. That particular sauce took forever to make, so I thought about cutting the steps down and using tomato paste, a little sauce with fresh basil for flavoring, and pasta water to add as a thickener, with only a finishing touch of cream at the end. All he did was shrug and say, "You had me at free dinner, Dakota."

I finished my coffee and went back inside, carefully locking the front door behind me. I took no chances these days.

There was still no sign of Poppy, so I filled her food and water bowl before heading to the back to get ready for the day. She'd come out when she was ready and not a moment before.

TWO

Copper Canyon was a scenic twenty-minute drive, and this early in the morning, it ended up being a pleasant distraction from my worries. A stainless-steel travel mug sat in the cup holder filled with hot coffee, and the radio played a soothing mix of southern folk. Humming along to the music, I turned onto the small side street where Georgia's shop was.

Page Turner's was the only bookstore in the small town. I hadn't been there yet, though I'd planned on stopping by soon. It was a standalone place, a two-story brick building with a small parking lot and numerous potted plants decorating the front of the shop. Georgia (or me for that matter), didn't have the same knack with the window display that Harriet did, but it was still adorably book themed.

It was fall, the leaves on the trees turning a stunning orange and red, lending the town a harvest-like feel.

Cinnamon and coffee scented the air when I slipped out of my vehicle, and I inhaled deeply before smiling. Fall was my favorite time of the year. Everything was a little better with hot cocoa and baked goods.

A cute wooden sign with the shop's name written in script hung above the door. A little pink and white book decorated the end. I stopped at the door, gawking at the lovely artwork before making a mental note to look into something similar. Tattered Pages had the shop name on the window. It looked good where it was, but hanging something above would make my shop easier to identify and add a decorative touch to the shop.

The door pushed open with a squeak, the sound of a tinkling bell announcing my arrival. A pretty woman at the register smiled and waved. "Dakota! Thanks so much for coming." She gestured for me to come inside.

"Hi, Georgia!" I stopped at the entrance and gaped. This place didn't look massive from the outside but being inside felt like stepping into a whole new world. Page Turner's smelled like vanilla and sandalwood, and books littered every single bit of available space. A few dozen shelves loomed high above, and just when I thought about asking how people reached the top of the shelves, I noticed ladders attached to each.

"You have ladders," I said faintly.

Georgia grinned. "Very Beauty and the Beast, I know, but I couldn't help myself. I wanted to carry as many books as possible, but I didn't have the space for all the extra shelves I needed."

It was a great idea, but... "What about liability?" I asked.

She pointed to each of the corners. "Cameras everywhere, and customers aren't actually allowed to use the ladders." Georgie pointed to a sign on one of the shelves. *Ladders are for employees only.* If I saw a ladder on a bookshelf, I'm not sure someone could stop me from riding the thing like Belle did in the library.

"How many times do you catch people?" I asked.

She laughed and rolled her eyes. "Too many times. The cameras stop most of them, but every once in a while, they get that gleam in their eye." Georgia's brows lifted. "Kind of like you have now."

"I'm not sure how much longer I can resist," I admitted.

Georgia snorted. "You are not a customer. Have a cup of coffee with me first, then you can ride the ladders."

"Deal!" I'd had enough coffee for a football team this morning, but one more wouldn't hurt.

GEORGIA LED me deeper into the store, past the romance and history sections, toward a small sitting area tucked away from the main store. The smell of coffee was stronger here. A large espresso machine sat on a table, a stack of paper travel cups with lids beside it.

"This is fancy for a bookstore," I said, "but I'm not complaining."

Georgia fussed with the machine, tamping the coffee

into a circle and adding extra water. "I'm a nut for coffee. There's nothing like drinking a fresh cup of well-made java early in the morning, is there?"

"Only if you get to sit on a nice porch with it," I admitted, taking a seat on a surprisingly comfortable chair.

She handed me the first cup, made hers, then joined me in a chair opposite. Both of us fell silent as we enjoyed the first few sips.

Georgia was right. This was an amazing cup of coffee. "Mmm," I said in appreciation.

"It's the beans," she said. "Delicious."

We sipped for a while, and I enjoyed the ambiance of her store and the yummy espresso. When I was halfway through, I studied her. "As much as I'm enjoying the star treatment, your email sounded urgent. Everything okay?"

Georgia sighed. "It's the shop. Someone is stealing from me."

I blinked. "A customer? Or an employee?"

She shook her head. "I'm not sure. I only have two employees, and they've both been with me for years. It seems like the most obvious explanation, but neither one of them would ever steal from me." Georgia rubbed her face. "I have regulars, but I know them all. Copper Canyon isn't a large town."

"If it's not a customer or an employee, who else could it be?" It didn't make any sense. "You have cameras everywhere, you said?"

She nodded. "I've been over the footage numerous times. Nothing is amiss."

"Have you called the police?" It seemed like an obvious first step, but maybe I was missing something.

Georgia grimaced. "Not yet. I wanted a second opinion from someone who knows books like I do."

I spread my hands. "I'm afraid I don't understand. How could I help you more than the police?"

"Whoever it is seems to be looking for something." She shook her head. "They're taking valuable books, but I can't help but think they haven't found what they're looking for yet."

"Which books?" Georgia's shop didn't focus as much on rare books as mine did, but she had a couple of locked cabinets with some goodies inside. She'd called me a few times since we met and asked a few questions about some purchases she wanted to make. Nothing extreme. A few special editions of *Harry Potter* and other YA books.

"I had a first edition of *Tom Sawyer* with the Morocco binding. Whoever it was swiped it first before they took anything else."

I winced. That book was ultra rare and worth over sixty grand. "Was it insured?"

Georgia blew out a breath. "Thankfully. I'd just bought a few more that weren't, though. They swiped those, too."

Ouch. "Does anyone have a key to the locked cabinet?"

"Just me and the manager. She's been with me since the beginning. There's no way she's involved." Georgia wrapped her hands around her mug and sighed.

"They took only rare books?"

"Packages, too."

"Let me guess. More books?"

She nodded. "But never from any of the main retailers." She shook her head. "It's odd. It's almost like whoever this is knows what I'm buying or recognizes the specific retailers and auction sites I purchase from."

"Was the case broken into?"

"No." Georgia inhaled a deep breath. "I only noticed because someone inquired about one of the books."

"So, no sign of forced entry." I chewed my bottom lip. "You've gone through the footage of every entry into the cabinet?"

"I have." Georgia groaned. "Mags never pulled out the stolen book. She only went into the cabinet a couple of times over the last two months. Our community isn't into the rare books as much as they are the second-hand copies." She shrugged. "I have them on hand mostly because I'm a collector. They don't often sell, and I get to look at them every day." Her cheeks colored. "That's probably silly."

I laughed. "Are you kidding? I'd snuggle with all my books every night if it wouldn't damage them."

Georgia laughed. "I'm glad I finally met someone who loves books as much as I do."

"I live and breathe them." Someone who was looking for something wouldn't stop until they found it. "Let's start with a list of everything this person has taken. I'll go through it and see if I can connect any dots."

Georgia nodded. "I'll email it to you later today."

I set my mug down. "In the meantime, I think you need to contact the police. You'll need a report for an insurance claim."

Georgia's eyes widened. "I didn't even think of that." She ran a hand over her face and groaned. "You're right. I'll do that as soon as we're finished here."

"They have resources I don't." Thoughts of Hardy sprang to mind, but I squashed them down. He didn't work in this town, so he wouldn't be the one responding to her call. "If the perpetrator sees a police force here, they might think twice about taking anything else."

I stood and picked my mug up.

"Oh, please," Georgia said. "Just leave it there. I'll put it in the dishwasher once I finish with mine."

I set it back down. "Appreciate it. Send me that email, and I'll take a look. Want to meet again in a few days? I'll bring donuts!"

"Definitely. How about Wednesday?" She opened her calendar and scrolled through the month. Ten?"

I did the same. "That will work. Any requests? The place I go to has amazing blueberry cake donuts."

"Oooh. I'll take a couple of those." She stood and picked up my cup. "Two, please. I'll have coffee ready to go."

"Sounds good." I waved and walked away, weaving through the shelves and admiring her vast selection of books as I let myself out. Her nonfiction selection was a little larger than her fiction, but Georgia knew her customers better than I ever could. Tattered Pages customers loved thrillers more than self-help and mysteries more than romance. I kept a small shelf of new releases and beloved romance favorites and had a note on the section about ordering any books a customer wanted. I couldn't get it there faster than a major corporation, but I'd have it to them within a few days.

When I left the store, I drove around Copper Canyon for a few minutes, mentally noting areas of interest I might want to explore later. A small bakery and a farmer's market posted a sign notifying customers it was open Sunday through Wednesday. I adored farmer's markets and made a mental note to add a couple of insulated shopping bags to my vehicle for the next time I came.

The construction crew would be at Tattered Pages in the next twenty minutes, so I turned my vehicle around and headed back to Silverwood Hollow.

THREE

I couldn't wait until construction was over. Bookstores were supposed to be quiet, and the constant clanging and banging was enough to drive a girl out of her mind. The door was already propped open, allowing the workers to get their tools and supplies in and out without someone holding the door open. It was cool enough for me to ignore it. During summer, I might have asked for them to keep it closed. Not that it was overly hot, but some days the humidity was enough of a concern I worried about damaged books.

The foreman was a tall, lanky man named Mitchell. I waved when I walked in, careful to watch where I stepped. They were working on an extra outer door today so they could stop using the main shop entrance.

I pointed at the frame, a hopeful expression on my face. "Will that be finished today?"

Mitchell laughed. He was used to my daily peppering of questions. "Yes, ma'am. The door is being delivered as we speak."

"Solid wood, right?"

"Solid mahogany, a small peephole. Everything you asked for, Miss Dakota."

The main bookstore door was glass, but this one was for the investigative agency, and I didn't want people peeping in. Gossip was a real problem in a small town; anyone who came in deserved their privacy. I'd tell potential customers to enter on the bookstore side to avoid suspicion. This door was mostly for me, but if a customer didn't care about any gossip, they were welcome to use it.

"Want a walk-through?" Mitch asked.

"I'd love one." Once I hung my sweater on the hook, I followed Mitch through the expansion, ignoring the pang in my heart as I remembered what the place used to be and where Trudy was now. So many things had changed since I opened my shop, and getting used to a new normal would take time.

He led me to the back office. "We just put the new flooring down and repaired the sheetrock. The lighting will be here tomorrow, so I think we should be able to install it if it arrives before lunch. The painters will be here the day after."

The wood was a beautiful dark color, protected by a thick sheet of hazy plastic. I lifted the edge of it and stroked the smooth but whorled surface. "Gorgeous," I murmured. "When do you think I can start putting furniture in?"

Mitch shrugged. "I wouldn't schedule anything for a week or two. I don't expect any delays, but I don't have control over shipping. Painters are notoriously late, too. I'll stay on top of everything and let you know if anything gets pushed."

"Thanks, Mitch." I had ordered a special antique desk with a large surface and several hidden compartments. The purchase had been a little frivolous, but it had felt right with the new investigative endeavor. A new filing cabinet with a biometric lock system was on the way, too.

He led me out of the office and down the hall toward a small kitchen. "The last owner left several items. We waited until her claim was over and added them to the design."

She'd left a nice stove, a large stainless refrigerator, and a gorgeous wooden chopping block built into a portable island. I ran my fingers over the scarred surface and wondered how many delectable things Trudy had created here. Guilt threatened to overwhelm me, and I took a couple of deep breaths. What Trudy had done wasn't my fault.

"How soon do you think I can open?"

Mitch shook his head. "A month or two, max. We're waiting on the rest of the flooring delivery. The painters can't finish their job until we finish all the repairs. Fortunately, you already have plumbing and electric installed.

Most are surface repairs and moving some things for a better layout. Turning a restaurant into an office is a bit of a challenge, but nothing we can't manage."

I exhaled. "It all looks great. Thanks so much."

Mitch smiled, transforming his face. It always took me by surprise when I saw it. He was a tall, lanky man, almost painfully thin. Mitch's expression remained serious ninety percent of the time, but when he smiled, it took my breath away. He was older, probably pushing late fifties, and I'd met his wife once. She was a pretty, short blonde with a ready smile and a mean chocolate chip cookie recipe.

"You're welcome, Miss Dakota. I'll send you an update when we finish for the day. I'm hoping the door will be here soon so we can shut the shop door for you. I have a couple of the crew sitting in the bookshop to keep customers from wandering in."

"Great." I shoved my hands in my pockets and wandered back into the bookstore. Several packages sat on top of the register area. Instead of leaving them for Monday, I took the boxes and loaded them into my vehicle, with a plan to go through them after I went to the grocery store. I still had time. Tonight's recipe I had in mind wouldn't take as long to cook as a normal Bolognese.

MY HANDS WERE full of packages when I stepped out of the shop. Navigating carefully through the maze of construction material, I stopped at the curb and set them down on the concrete.

Cole, my friend and local reporter, shouted a hello and jogged over. "Let me get that," he said, taking my keys from me and loading everything into the trunk.

While he did that, I ducked back into the shop and grabbed my sweater.

Cole was closing up the trunk when I came back out, shrugging my arms into my sweater.

"I haven't seen you in forever," I exclaimed.

Cole grinned and pushed his wire-framed glasses up on his nose. "I was over in Copper Canyon covering a story." He opened his arms for a hug. I stepped into them and inhaled the fresh scent of his cologne. His arms tightened for a brief moment. "How have you been?" he murmured against my hair before letting go. Cole knew about Hardy. I rarely had to tell the man anything. He had a knack for ferreting information out before anyone else was the wiser. It didn't help that the two had never gotten along. Not exactly. They were friendlyish but not friends.

"I've been good." It was mostly true. "Things are getting busy with the construction." I gestured toward the shop. "Mitch said I could move in maybe in a month or two."

His eyes widened. "Wow! That's awesome." Cole tapped his shirt pocket where his ever-trusty notepad lay. "How about a story to help you drum up some business?"

"I'd love that. I'll keep you posted."

"Good." He shifted on his feet and cleared his throat. "Dakota—"

I snorted. Cole still felt guilty about telling me about

Hardy. "I would have found out anyway. You know I would have. If not from you, the Silverwood Silverettes would have started a phone tree."

His smile didn't meet his eyes. "I know. It doesn't make it better, though. How are you really doing?"

My shoulders slumped. "Heartbroken," I admitted.

Cole's mouth turned down. "Dakota."

"No. It's—I'm getting better. Every single day makes it hurt a little less."

He exhaled. "If it makes you feel better, Hardy looks awful."

A surprised laugh bubbled from my lips. "Thanks, Cole."

We grinned at each other. He put a hand on my shoulder. "If you need anything at all, give me a call. Maybe we can do lunch soon."

"I'd love that. Daniel is coming over for dinner tonight, so I'm not alone."

His brows lifted in surprise. "He still cheating at chess?"

I nodded. "Still totally unrepentant about it, too."

Cole laughed. "You'll figure it out."

"I won't tell him when I do. But I will raise the stakes."

"Oooh. Try to get two copies of his next book so we can both have one."

"Will do." Daniel had a new book slated for release three months from now. He'd already promised me a large shipment to sell in the store, but I still hoped to wrangle a few advance copies out of him.

Cole handed my keys back. "I hope one of those is my new journal," he said, pointing at the trunk.

"No idea. I didn't even look at the return addresses. I'll drop it by the Gazette if it is."

"You're the best, Dakota!" he said and turned to go. "Lunch next week. I'll call you."

"Sounds good."

I watched him walk away, glad we'd been able to repair our friendship before it was past the point of no return. Shaking my head, I got into my vehicle and drove away.

It was still relatively early, so traffic was light. It took half the normal time to get to the grocery store. My heart-beat picked up speed when I noticed a police cruiser in the parking lot. The odds of it being Hardy were low but not zero, so I sat in my vehicle for a few minutes hoping whoever it was would come out.

When no one did, I sighed and got out. I was an adult. We lived in the same town. It was inevitable I'd run into him again.

I didn't want to, but it wasn't something I could avoid forever.

I took a small shopping cart and headed inside, making a beeline for the produce department.

I spotted him ten minutes into my trip. Broad shoulders, dark hair, chiseled jawline. I'd know him anywhere. My heart skittered to a halt, and tears filled my eyes. A lump formed in my throat, and I stood there, stopped in the middle of the aisle, and staring.

His hair had grown out a little and was more mussed

than usual. Before he could spot me, I forced myself to turn my basket around and hurry out of the aisle. Dashing away the tears falling down my cheek, I inhaled and exhaled, trying to calm my hammering heartbeat.

They said time healed all wounds, but this one felt like it would always be open and raw. Honestly, Hardy and I were like electricity and water. He didn't like me getting involved with his investigations and had never made a secret about it. Hardy was the kind of man who would be overprotective about everything rather than give someone the freedom to make their own mistakes, but there was so much about him that was open and giving and loving.

But there was no way to come back from what happened. Not that I could see. And that was okay. The longer I spent away from him, the better I felt. Granted, seeing him today felt like someone stabbed me in the heart, but even that would fade.

I hoped.

I spent ten minutes toward the back of the store, poking through the freezer section and keeping a vigilant eye out for Hardy's tall frame.

When I felt safe that he was gone, I hurried up, grabbed the rest of the things on my list, and checked out.

I'd just finished loading the trunk of my car when a shadow fell over me. I jerked in surprise and looked up.

Hardy stood over me.

My mouth fell open, and I slowly straightened, clicking the trunk shut.

He stared at me, those once devilish blue eyes haunted. "You're avoiding me." His voice was raspy and hoarse.

What could I say? Of course I was avoiding him. "Can you blame me?" I said after a long, awkward pause.

He shut his eyes for a moment and exhaled a long breath. "No." Hardy ran a hand through his mussed hair. "How can we get past this?"

All the words on my lips dried up. How can you get past someone you loved so much it took your breath away? I let him go because he deserved the opportunity to see where this thing went. He had a child. A history I wasn't a part of.

I shook my head, mute. "Time," I finally croaked.

"I don't want time, Dakota." He clenched his jaw and looked away. "I want you."

"Hardy. Please. Don't do this." The keys shook in my hand.

"She's gone," he said.

I blinked. "Gone?"

"She left without...Molly."

"Oh." I leaned against the trunk. "Molly is her name?"

He nodded, love flashing in his eyes.

"That's a cute name."

"Yeah," he agreed.

Silence fell between us.

"Why did she leave?"

Hardy shrugged. "I don't think she ever had any intention of staying once I made it clear I wouldn't pick back up where we left things."

"I'm sorry to hear that, Hardy."

He snorted. "I'm not. We weren't good for each other. But Molly is suffering. I can't find her mom to communicate how this is affecting her." Hardy shook his head. "It's been difficult, but she's settling in okay, I think."

"That's good." What could I say to him? There was nothing left to say. Just because she left didn't mean we could just jump back into the place we were when they'd shown up. He needed time to adjust to having a child.

And I...well, I wasn't prepared for what any of that meant.

"You'll be a good father," I said and pushed away from the trunk.

When Hardy realized I was leaving, he reached for me, his warm hand clasping my forearm.

I looked down at it and back up at him.

"I—I don't know what the future looks like, Dakota. But I know I miss you every single day. I want you back in my life."

I shook my head. "I'm sorry. I can't. Not right now."

"Even if it's as a friend. I know things are messed up between us, but I can't bear the thought of not seeing you again, not talking to you. Everything is broken between us, and I don't know if I can fix it, but I want to try."

I pulled my arm away. "It's too soon. You need time to adjust to your new normal, especially now that she...her mom, is gone. And I can't pretend to want to be friends with you when we were once something so much more." I shook my head. "For now, please just...let me be."

Turning away from Hardy broke my heart all over again, but I unlocked the door and slid into my vehicle, waiting for him to step away. I didn't look in the rearview when I drove away.

Sometimes, all you could do was look ahead.

FOUR

The not Bolognese sauce turned out amazing. Daniel had two bowls and went back for a little more, cleaning me out of any leftover potential before the night was through.

We were halfway through our second game when Daniel checkmated me again.

"Aaaaargh!" I blew out an annoyed breath.

Poppy's head jerked up from Daniel's thigh. If cats could glare, Poppy's look would have burned through my soul. Her head plopped back down, and she snuggled closer to him.

"Honestly, Dakota. I'm not even cheating. What's going on with you?" Daniel's dark, serious gaze rested on my face. He was interested in more than friendship but respectful of my hesitation, and he'd never once pressed me, especially after what happened with Hardy.

He was my friend, but he was also something more. Something I wasn't prepared to deal with right now.

"I ran into Hardy earlier."

Daniel's brows lifted. "Ah. How did that go?"

I shook my head. "I don't think we should talk about it."

Daniel laughed. "Dakota, we've been through a lot together. I'm a friend, aren't I?"

My eyes narrowed, making Daniel laugh.

He pressed a hand against his heart. "I am. We might not have the most traditional friendship, but we've been meeting for chess and dinner for months now, haven't we?"

"We have," I said warily.

"I know your heart is broken," he said solemnly. "It's written all over your face. I will be here no matter what you decide. If chess is the only thing you want, chess is the only thing you shall have." His smile deepened. "I am an extreme introvert. These chess nights are the only thing that get me out of the house. You'll have to pry my chess pieces from my cold dead fingers, Dakota." He cleared the board and set it up again. "Now tell me what else the insufferable Hardy Cavanaugh did to you."

I laughed and helped him set up another match. Daniel was right. Our friendship wasn't traditional, but it worked, which didn't mean I was completely comfortable telling him about Hardy, so I skimmed over most of it, only telling him about Molly staying with Hardy full-time. I also told him about her mother leaving, conveniently leaving out how it made me feel.

From the amused curve of his lips, he knew what I was doing, but he didn't call me on it. "He wants you back?"

I shook my head. "No. I—I don't think so. He wants us to go back to the way we were, I think."

Daniel stared at me. "The way you were was back together," he said gently.

"I think he doesn't want the tension between us." I buried my head in my hands. "It's all so complicated."

"I have empathy for him," Daniel said, surprising the heck out of me.

My face must have betrayed my thoughts. He laughed at my expression and lifted his hands in surrender.

"I do! It's not every day someone you haven't seen for years comes and drops a bomb on your life like she did. What happened was unfair to Hardy and his child."

It really was. As much as what happened had blown my life up, it was nothing compared to how having a child he didn't know of affected Hardy. I reached over and touched his hand. "Thank you, Daniel."

"I'm not finished." He took my hand and held it. "While I do have empathy for his situation, it's inappropriate for him to approach you like that. He broke your heart. It doesn't seem like he's fixed anything, and now with the child's mother gone, he's drowning. You are a bright spot for him, Dakota. You always have been. Of course, he wants you back. He'd be an idiot not to, but I'm not sure it's for the right reasons. Not yet anyway."

I tried to pull my hand back, but he held on. "No matter what you decide, I'll support you. Being your friend doesn't come with strings or conditions."

My heart warmed at that, even though his words

angered me. And not because they were wrong. In my heart, I knew Daniel was right. I just wasn't ready to hear it.

"All I want is your happiness." He squeezed my hand and let me go. "And if it's with him, so be it. But maybe give this more time before you try to have any type of relationship. Everything is raw. He's never been a father before." Daniel shrugged and chuckled. "I haven't either, but I don't think something like that is like riding a bike. Maybe more like learning physics as an adult when you've forgotten most of your high school math."

Everything he said was true, but every word felt like a dart to the heart. All I could do was nod. When I finished setting up my side of the chess board, I gestured at him to begin. "Tonight's the night I figure out how you're cheating," I said, hoping he would take the hint and let me change the subject.

Fortunately, he did. He moved his Knight first. "You think I'm cheating, but it's only because I'm excellent at chess and you are terrible."

I gasped in false outrage. "Lies," I mockingly hissed. He wasn't wrong. I was terrible at chess, but I wasn't as bad as he made me out to be.

Daniel Jensen *was* cheating, and I'd figure out how eventually.

AFTER SOUNDLY BEATING me in four more games, we both gave up. Daniel took his consolation prize—a dozen homemade chocolate chip cookies, but he left me the fancy bottle of wine he brought, so I probably made out better in the end.

Once his headlights disappeared down the road, I locked the door behind me, double-checked it, and poured myself another glass before heading into the living room. We cleaned up the chess board before he left and pushed it to the side of the coffee table. I'd put it up later.

My email dinged just as I set my glass down. Instead of looking at it on my phone, I pulled my laptop over, settled on the couch, and opened it up.

Georgia's name sat at the top of the unread pile. The subject matter said *Missing Books*. There was no greeting, only a short list of all the books and packages stolen from her shop.

I skimmed the list and noticed nothing alarming right away. She listed the *Tom Sawyer* book, and even though I already knew it was gone, I felt another stab of empathy for Georgia. Not only was that book ridiculously expensive, but it was also rare, and a fantastic find. Some people might consider something like that just a book, but we were collectors. Few manuscripts were *just* books in our world.

I spent weeks, sometimes months searching for certain books, even if I couldn't afford them. Just knowing they were out there, that people still treasured them, gave me the warm fuzzies.

She had a first edition of *Animal Farm*, worth over six grand, and a first edition of *The Hobbit*, worth somewhere around the fifty grand mark. The others were smaller collectibles, somewhere in the low hundreds to a few thousand dollars.

All of them, however, were classics.

Below the list, Georgia wrote a short paragraph.

Strangely enough, I'm missing several copies of illustrated bird books. One is Birds of Britain, another is The Migration of Birds. Both are worth over fifty bucks, but they aren't as expensive as the others. I'm missing about eight books about birds in total.

Bird books? Odd. I sent the email to my printer to look at later, then jumped on Google to search some of the titles she was missing. The ornithology books were a little strange, and there were more of those missing than any others. None of the other stolen books had anything in common other than being classics. I did another search for rare and valuable bird books and sucked in a breath when I stumbled across a four-volume set of The Birds of America, illustrated by John Audubon.

Only thirteen copies remained, all in private hands, and the most recent auction of one went over nine million dollars.

I blew out a breath and settled back into the couch cushions. Nine *million* bucks?

That couldn't be what the thief was after. If all these copies were in private hands, why would the thief think Georgia would have one? She had a small, local bookstore in a town with a population of only a few thousand. There was nothing notable about Copper Canyon—no eccentric collectors or rich heiresses. Granted, I'd only just met Georgia, but she didn't specialize in rare books. After going to her store today, I noticed she only had a couple in her display cases, nothing to justify the amount of theft she'd received over the last couple of months.

It had to be something else.

But another question kept teasing the back of my mind. Georgia's shop was relatively new in town. Her background was unknown to me. Maybe she came from money or had accrued wealth in a former career. Maybe she'd wisely invested. How could she afford the rare books she was purchasing and why was Georgia, specifically, being targeted? There were too many other shops with much better selections to target, so what did she have that appealed to thieves more than the other places?

Shaking my head, I closed my laptop and put it to the side. I had a few days before Georgia and I met again, and it was getting late.

I had a free day tomorrow and planned to use it doing nothing except hanging out at the house and experimenting in the kitchen.

Smiling to myself, I reached for my wineglass. In spite of everything going on and how quiet the house had become these last few months, being alone and basking in the quiet wasn't as bad as I thought it might be.

FIVE

Two dozen chocolate chip cookies sat cooling on a large rack in the middle of my kitchen island. A cup of steaming cappuccino sat beside it. I'd woken up early this morning, did some quick weeding in the front landscaping bed, showered, and gone straight into the kitchen and started baking.

The construction crew was off today. Tattered Pages was closed, and I had no errands to run. Mom and Gran were due over sometime this afternoon for a visit. I hadn't seen them for a week. A lot could happen in a week when it came to those two. I slipped my apron over my head, hanging it on the hook by the back door. The cookies had cooled just enough for the edges to get the crispy texture I loved, so I snagged one and carried it and my cappuccino over to the table.

Georgia's plight had been on my mind all morning long. Mom and Gran were great sounding boards and had occasionally stepped up to help me out with cases. Maybe they could help me figure out if there was a link between any of the missing books and set me at ease with my curiosity over Georgia obtaining those expensive books.

But until they got here, I had a cookie and a cappuccino to enjoy.

MY FAMILY BLEW through the door two hours later. Gran's hair looked freshly dyed, the red color bringing out the creamy paleness of her skin. She held out her arms and brought me into a floral scented hug. Mom came up behind her and soon it was a triple Adair hug. The best kind of hug.

When we let go, I led them back to the kitchen and served up cookies and coffee. Mom had a weakness for my chocolate chip cookies, and Gran never passed on any food she didn't have to make. I snagged a second cookie and took the reading chair so they could take the couch.

After the first bite, Mom spoke. "How are you, honey?"

She packed a lot of meaning in those few words. When everything with Hardy blew up, Mom was the first to lend a shoulder. I could only hope if I ever had children, I'd be as good to them as she'd been to me.

"I'm good. I promise."

Gran munched on her cookie. "Heard you had a guest last night." She wiggled her eyebrows like a lecher.

"Not like that," I muttered, rolling my eyes.

"That Daniel boy," Gran said to Mom. "Handsome,

intelligent, and famous!" She pretended like she was waving a hand fan at her face. "You can't go wrong with a triple threat like that."

Mom snorted. "Well, there you go, Dakota. When do we start planning the wedding?" The look in her eyes was sympathetic. She was amazing, but she wanted grandkids. Considering my love life was grounded until further notice, it might be a long while until her prayers were answered. If ever. I still wasn't sure if kids were in the cards for me, or if I truly wanted them.

Mom was a little more grounded and patient about it, and I knew if I came up to her and told her I decided things would stay the way they were, she'd have a moment of sadness, but she'd respect it. Gran might have an aneurysm. They were mom and daughter, but Gran was a firecracker, and Mom was more of a winter, crackling fire—strong and steady.

I loved them both to pieces, though.

"We play chess once a week, Gran. That's it."

Gran leaned forward and peered at me with piercing blue eyes. "Is chess a euphemism for something?"

Mom blew out a breath and took Gran's mug. "I think you should switch to decaf," she muttered under her breath as she walked to the kitchen.

"Daniel is just a friend," I emphasized, waiting while Mom made a new pot of coffee. Decaf, this time. Probably for the best. If I put on a pot of coffee, I'd drink every single bit of it and be as wired as a power line.

"I'm glad you're both here," I said when Mom settled back onto the couch.

"Wait!" Mom said. "First tell us how the construction is going on the expansion." When I told her what I was doing, she was a little apprehensive, but mostly elated. Mom liked me having the bookstore, but she was still on the fence about a PI business. When I told her I had no plans to take on murder cases or anything terribly dangerous, she'd relaxed some, but then made the valid point of how I had yet to have a single safe case since I started looking into things for people.

Then Gran had chimed in and said I'd probably do a better job than the police, and I was so glad Hardy hadn't been there. That was one of the things that set our relationship on a downhill slide. We were starting to get past his stubbornness about me getting involved in investigations, but looking back, I wondered if the issue would have kept cropping its head up over and over again until it eventually broke us.

I couldn't dwell in the past while expecting to go forward. Shaking my head to clear those thoughts, I smiled at Mom. "Great. They think everything will be finished in a month or two. I haven't applied for a business license or anything yet, and I think I have to be licensed to operate as a PI in the state." Shrugging, I took a sip of my coffee. "For now, the extra space will stay empty until I figure everything out."

Mom studied me. "Are you afraid of venturing into something else?"

I thought about it. That question had kept me up some nights, wondering if I was crazy to even consider trying to become a private investigator. "A little, I think. Mostly I wonder if I'll still have time for the bookstore if I open up a PI firm."

"You have Harper," Gran reminded me.

"I do," I assured her. "And she's wonderful. Sometimes I miss being just a bookseller, though." My cases had kept me out of the shop quite often, leaving Harper to pick up the slack. She didn't mind and turned out to have quite the head for business. I rewarded her for it with raises and perks, but the bookstore was mine, and I wasn't completely ready yet to hand over the day-to-day operations to someone else.

"Sometimes our passions and talents collide," Gran said gently. "You love books, but you have a knack for solving mysteries. There's nothing wrong with either. If you can afford to do both, you should give it a whirl. Life's too short to be afraid of trying new things."

Warmth bloomed in my chest. Gran always knew the right thing to say. "Thanks, Gran."

She winked at me. "Got any more cookies?"

Mom laughed and got up to bring the plate over. "That's why she made two dozen, you little glutton."

Gran cracked a laugh and reached for another cookie. "The difference is I'll eat two and you'll eat twelve." She popped a bite in her mouth, chewed, and grabbed one more for good measure.

"Who's the glutton now," Mom said with a laugh. But I noticed Mom took two more, too.

Glad I made a couple dozen. I didn't tell them I had more dough in the fridge.

"Now tell us what's going on," Mom said.

I explained about Georgia and how I'd met her, leading into the thefts in her shop. Mom asked to see the list. Gran scooted over and peered at it with Mom. After a moment, Gran frowned. "Birds?"

I'd scribbled notes all over the place. Mom tapped the paper. "Birds of Audubon?" She whistled low. "I saw something in the news about that book. Some kind of auction where it went for millions. You think there's a link?"

I sighed. "It's too soon to tell. The first few thefts look unrelated."

"Crime of opportunity," Gran said.

"Georgia insists she and only one other person had a key to the cabinet, and she's adamant the woman wouldn't take anything from her. They've worked together for years."

Mom grimaced. "I'd like to think the same thing, but money can do terrible things to someone."

"Can you discreetly look into the worker?" Gran added. "See if there's anything concerning about her. If you don't find anything, then put it aside for now. But if something comes back, you can keep digging."

"That green-eyed fellow can help you," Mom said. "What's his name? Colby?"

"Cole." He had connections all over the country. I chewed on my lip. "He's going to get nosy about it, though." We'd had issues in the beginning of our relationship where Cole was more interested in the story than my well-being. Things were better now, but Cole would never lose his hunter instinct when it came to breaking news.

"You're friends, aren't you? There's no story there yet." Gran sipped her decaf and grimaced. She slid a look over to Mom. "Is this really how you treat me in my golden years? With decaf?"

Mom rolled her eyes. "I have to ride home with you, and you're like a yappy Chihuahua when you've had more than one cup of regular coffee."

Gran huffed but didn't disagree. It didn't stop her from trying to steal Mom's coffee when she wasn't looking, though.

I brought the conversation back around. "We are friends. Cole won't have the same tools as Hardy, but he may know someone who does."

"Then start there," Mom said. "Just to rule out the most obvious person. You never know where it might lead you."

It was good advice. Start with the most obvious solution and go from there.

"I'll shelve the bird book theory for now."

Mom snorted at my book pun. "You'll figure it out, honey. You always do."

Gran stood and stretched. "How about I cook us dinner?"

"I vote for Italian meatloaf!" I said. It wasn't quite meatloaf, and it wasn't quite Italian. It tasted like Salisbury steak with Italian herbs. Gran always made it with delicious roasted potatoes and glazed carrots.

Mom waved her hand. "Dakota wins. You haven't made that in a while, and she did make us cookies."

Gran brushed past me and dropped a kiss on top of my hair. "Dakota always wins because she's the cutest."

Mom barked a laugh. "Grandkids always win," she grumbled.

I grinned at them both and curled my feet under me.

Having them here always relaxed me.

Especially when I didn't have to make dinner.

SIX

Cole sat across from me, blond hair ruffling in the wind. He wore a grey sweater and an emerald-colored scarf, bringing out the green in his eyes. Next to him sat the familiar scarred leather satchel he used to carry his laptop and notebook.

We sat outside at a little cafe on the border between Silverwood and Copper Canyon. The temps were a little too cool to be eating outside, but there was a half an hour wait to get inside. They had heaters lined up every few rows, and it was surprisingly toasty.

His lips curved into a rueful smile. "Can't say I'm surprised to see you getting involved in another mystery."

"Georgia asked me to help," I said primly. "I couldn't tell her no."

"You couldn't?" Cole asked, his eyebrows lifting in amusement.

I scoffed. "Not when it comes to books!"

He laughed. "I'm just messing with you. If anyone can figure it out, it's you."

The server came over to refresh our coffee. When she left, Cole leaned over and took his leather-bound notebook out, sliding the pen from its slot and jotted something down. "What do you need?"

I explained about Georgia and her employee, and the thefts she'd been experiencing. Last night, I emailed her and asked her for the names of her employees. She provided them, but reiterated she didn't think either of them were involved. Though I assured her it was only routine, I still had to rule them out before moving forward.

"Can you run background checks on these two people?" I slid a piece of paper with the info over to him. "These are Georgia's employees."

Cole's gaze skimmed over the list. "You think they're involved?"

"Georgia doesn't. I'm trying to be thorough."

Cole reached for his laptop.

"You can do it now?" I asked in surprise.

Cole grinned. "New tools." He waved his hand over the keyboard. "That's all I can tell you." He slid the list over and typed something. "I'll have something for you before the entrees come out."

I people-watched while Cole tapped away on his laptop, his brow furrowing the more he searched.

"Everything okay?" I asked when his lips pursed.

He blinked and jerked his eyes up to me. "Oh. Yes. Just some odd things. I can't find one of these employees."

I scooted my chair over and peered around at his computer. Cole didn't try to hide it this time. "Which one?" I asked.

"Kelsie Smith. The other one has a clear background." He shrugged. "A pending speeding ticket. Nothing unusual."

"Smith. Common enough name, but easy to fake," I said.

"Do you have a picture of her?"

I shook my head. Georgia might have one but— "Oh! Check her website. Georgia mentioned they've been with her for a while, so maybe she has pictures of them there."

Cole typed in the site address and pulled up Georgia's online store. "Go to the About page," I instructed.

Cole's lips quirked up. "I think I got it, Dakota."

I held up my hands. "Sorry. I get excited when I get curious."

He laughed and clicked on the icon. It brought up Georgia's picture and bio, followed by photos of Melissa Garcia, the manager, and Kelsie.

Cole right clicked on the photo and saved it to his computer. Curious, I watched everything he was doing. He pulled up another website, uploaded Kelsie's photo, and clicked on Reverse Image Search.

"Ooh. What are you doing?"

"You can take any picture, upload it here, and see if there are any matches online."

"Matches?"

"Yes. If she uploaded this photo anywhere else, this

program should be able to find it online." He shrugged. "It's not a hundred percent, but it works more often than not. Sometimes you can right click on the photo from the website it's on and find an option to search it through Google, but not all sites are equipped for those searches yet."

A whole page of pictures popped up, several of them the same one Cole found on Georgia's site.

"What in the world?" I muttered, leaning closer to Cole.

He clicked the first one. It brought him to one of those stock photo sites. I slumped in my seat. "Great."

"Yup," Cole agreed. "It could mean a lot of things. She might be in hiding."

"Or she could be the one stealing from Georgia. Or worse."

Cole nodded and shut his laptop. "The first thing I'd do is call Georgia and let her know."

"I'm due there later today. I'd rather tell her in person."

"If she's amenable to it, ask her about adding some hidden cameras." He tucked his laptop back into his brief-case. "Sometimes the culprit is the one right in front of you."

"It would make it a lot easier if Kelsie was the thief," I agreed.

The server came with our food, cutting off any further talk of thieves or investigations.

Fine by me. The chicken was to die for.

Page Turner's was busy when I showed up, so I slipped

in while Georgia was preoccupied with customers. She was due to close in less than ten minutes. The mystery section bustled with people, mostly older women. I browsed, moving closer to the group, and scoping out good places to hide cameras. Several promising nooks and crannies presented themselves, and I made mental notes as I walked.

The conversation was about new releases and old favorites, so I listened with half an ear while I waited for Georgia to finish up. An announcement came over the loudspeaker a few minutes later asking everyone to move to the register and finalize their purchases.

I browsed for a little while longer, peeking around shelves to see how many customers were left. There were no other employees working today, but she was almost finished, so I made my way back to the business section.

The bell over the door jingled, announcing the last customer's exit. I rounded a corner and stopped abruptly. Two kitten-heeled feet lay on the ground, the rest of the person obscured by shelving.

I exhaled, my heart thundering through my ears.

As I stepped around the corner, a familiar face revealed itself.

Unfortunately, I suspected I'd just found the body of Kelsie Smith.

SEVEN

Georgia smiled when she saw me, offering a small wave before she brushed her forearm against her forehead.

"Whoo!" she said in greeting. "Such a busy day." A frown marred her smooth brow. "Kelsie came in, but I haven't seen her for at least an hour!" Georgia shook her head. "She must have left early, but it's unlike her not to tell me."

I didn't have the heart to tell her maybe she should add more mysteries to her catalog and cut down on the business books. "About that," I said gently, "we need to call the police."

Georgia's face fell. She straightened. "The police? Why?"

I hated breaking news like this. Sometimes, being a bookseller was all the excitement I ever wanted or needed.

I pulled my cellphone out. "I found Kelsie."

Georgia gasped. "What? Where?"

I dialed 911 and told the dispatcher what I found. When they asked about CPR, I informed them Kelsie was past the point of resuscitation efforts.

A broken sob escaped Georgia. She rushed out from behind the desk before I could grab her arm.

"We have officers on the way, ma'am. Please stay where you are."

I disconnected and headed after Georgia.

We sat on the store's small porch a few minutes later. Georgia buried her head in her arms and sat hunched over herself. Sirens came a short time later, one ambulance and a police car with an unmarked vehicle behind it, rushing through town.

I stood, brushing off the seat of my pants, and jogged down the stairs to wait.

The unmarked car pulled in first. To my horror, Hardy Cavanaugh stepped out of the vehicle.

Why in the world was he here? Blood rushed through my veins. I stood up straighter, resisting the urge to flee. When he spotted me, his eyes flickered before his expression went blank.

"Dakota," he said, his voice almost a growl. "Why am I not surprised to see you here?"

It was the same old thing, but I didn't react to his question. "She's inside. Do you need me to show you where?"

Hardy didn't say anything for a long moment. His gaze flicked to the building. "Please."

Without another word, I turned and led him inside. Hardy's presence burned at my back, but all the words I wanted to say dried up in my throat. Instead, I choked down my grief, walking through the silent bookstore until I rounded the corner where Kelsie lay.

He stepped in front of me, one hand out to keep me behind him. His hand hovered over his weapon. "Stay back," he warned. Two police officers came up behind us, sweeping out to either side of the bookshelf.

I took a few steps back before turning to go back outside and wait. None of them needed me for what was to come, but I knew they'd have some questions when they finished.

Georgia sat in the same position, head buried in her arms. I sat beside her and laid a hand on her shoulder. "They'll be in there for a while. I'll wait here with you until they're finished. I'm sure the officers will have questions for both of us."

She drew in a shaky sigh. "I didn't see anything. How long was I behind the register completely oblivious to whatever Kelsie was going through?"

My heart hurt for her. "None of this is your fault. Let's see what the police say before we jump to conclusions."

Georgia lifted her head, red-rimmed eyes studying me. "Could you tell what happened to her?"

"No." She looked like she was sleeping. "I saw no evidence of any physical violence, Georgia. It could be anything. Even natural causes."

"She was healthy as a horse," Georgia mumbled. "Kelsie never took a single sick day."

I'd forgotten about my lunch with Cole. "There's something else," I said gently.

Georgia's eyes fluttered shut. Her nostrils flared. "What is it?"

"I took the liberty of looking into your employees."

Her eyes opened wide. "What? Why?"

"A routine peek," I assured her. "It's easiest to rule out the most obvious suspects."

"Is Melissa safe?"

I blinked. That was an odd question. "I can't say, but her identity checked out. Kelsie's did not."

Georgia frowned. "I ran background checks on both of them. Both came back clean."

Cole's software must dig deeper. "I have a friend who ran a more intense check. Kelsie Smith, at least *your* Kelsie, does not exist."

She shook her head in disbelief. "I can't imagine she is guilty. Kelsie—" she stopped, "or whatever her name is, worked for me for years. Her registers always balanced perfectly, to the penny. Melissa had been here longer and did a great job for me, so I offered her the position instead of Kelsie. That's the only reason I chose Melissa over her. Both are model employees."

"Did she ever say anything about her past? Anything that might lead you to believe she was running from something?"

Georgia paused, her brow furrowing in thought. "She mentioned a boyfriend a long time ago. I don't think it ended well. But there wasn't anything that sent up red flags. Maybe I wasn't perceptive enough."

"Never think that. Sometimes the people we trust the most are the best at deceiving us." My heart cracked a little more. "Even if they don't mean to."

Georgia made a noise of assent. "The police should be able to identify her, right?"

"I hope so." If I could find out who Kelsie really was, it might help lead us to the real thief. "Dental records would do it, I think."

We sat together in silence for a while until the front door opened. Hardy stepped out with one of the uniformed officers, his gaze flicking over us before gesturing to the other officer to go ahead. With a gesture I'd seen far too many times, Hardy flipped open his jacket and pulled out a small notebook and a pen. He walked down a few steps, turned and sat down, facing us.

"Miss Macintosh," Hardy said. "I'm sorry to meet under these circumstances."

Georgia dipped her head. "Detective Cavanaugh, I presume?"

My brow furrowed. They seemed familiar with each other. I tamped down my curiosity. Now wasn't the time for it.

"I have a few questions for you both. We can do this now or you can come to the station tomorrow." Those devastating blue eyes met mine.

Georgia rubbed a hand over her face. "Can I come in

tomorrow, please? I actually don't know much. Dakota is the one who found her."

Hardy gave me a long look. "That's fine, Miss MacIntosh."

"Georgia, please." She rose to her feet and tugged her cardigan closer.

"Georgia, then." He dug in his jacket pocket and handed her the business card he pulled out. "I'll meet you at the Copper Canyon Police Station tomorrow at ten a.m. That time work for you?"

She nodded and took the card. "Tomorrow, then."

Hardy dipped his head. "Go on home."

Georgia walked down the steps slowly and turned right, her head lowered and shoulders hunched.

Hardy let out a deep sigh and scrubbed his palm against his jaw. "Dakota—" he began.

"Georgia asked me to look into some book thefts at her store," I interrupted. "I came here a few days ago and then again today. Georgia was busy with customers, and I was browsing through the store when I walked into the business section. That's where I found Kelsie's body."

He gave me a long look before putting pen to paper. When he finished writing, I didn't let him start talking. "I found out that Kelsie Smith is an alias."

His eyes jerked from the paper up to me. "How?"

"Doesn't matter. The other employee, Melissa Garcia, checked out. Georgia was unaware of anything in Kelsie's past that might have explained her false identity and seems adamant neither woman would have been involved in the thefts."

"Dakota," he warned.

"It doesn't matter," I said again. "What matters is there's a dead woman with a false identity lying in Georgia's store and a history of expensive rare book thefts."

When Hardy didn't react, a thought occurred to me. "You know about the thefts, don't you?"

Hardy's lips quirked up. "Doesn't matter."

Touché.

"How long will her bookstore be closed?"

Hardy shrugged. "Depends. Once officers clear the scene and process the evidence, Georgia will be allowed back in."

"I'd like to set up cameras."

One of his eyebrows rose. "Why?"

"To catch a thief. If Kelsie wasn't involved, there's still a thief out there. Now is the perfect time to set up surveillance." I frowned. "Unfortunately."

"You can't go into the crime scene. I have no authority to grant permission. You'll have to go through Georgia once the store is reopened."

I figured I'd have to anyway, but I had four cameras in my bag, purchased right after I'd eaten lunch with Cole. If I could get back in and set them up while no one was there, it would be less suspicious. Of course, I'd let Georgia know, but I knew, just like always, I was on thin ice with Hardy.

I shrugged. "Fair enough."

Hardy gave me a suspicious look before returning his

attention to his notebook. He scribbled a few more things before snapping it shut, tucking the pen back into the spiral, and putting it back into his jacket pocket.

"Why are you here?" I asked.

He blinked. "Excuse me?"

"You don't work for Copper Canyon. You work for Silverwood. Or has something changed?"

"Dakota, I no longer owe you any information. You've made that clear."

With those parting words, Hardy rose and walked away.

EIGHT

The police didn't clear out for hours. When I started getting suspicious glances from a few of the officers, I figured I should cut my losses and skedaddle. Sneaking into a crime scene with officers on the scene was the height of idiocy, and I liked to think I was usually pretty smart.

I headed back to the car and went home, my thoughts swirling over the day's events.

Seeing Hardy again so soon was bad enough, but I was working in this town under the assumption I wouldn't see him at all for the foreseeable future. To see him after finding a body again felt like the height of déjàvu.

"Ugh," I muttered. Why couldn't I get away from him?

When I stopped at a red light, I dialed Georgia and activated the Bluetooth.

She answered on the first ring. "Dakota? Everything okay?"

"Hi. I'm calling first to check on you."

"I'm okay." Her sigh was heavy. "I just can't believe she's gone."

"I'm so sorry. I know this is awful for you. But trust that Hardy is on the case. He's an excellent detective. If someone hurt Kelsie, he will find them."

There was a long silence. "You seem confident in him. Do you know him?"

Georgia and I hadn't known each other long. Apparently, word of my investigative exploits had not reached Copper Canyon. Something that sent relief spearing through me.

"Uh, yes. We briefly dated, but we have a friendly relationship now." It wasn't quite a lie. Hardy and I didn't hate each other, but we certainly wouldn't be having chess nights anytime soon.

"Ah," Georgia said. "That explains those heavy looks he was giving you." She huffed a short laugh. "I'm okay. There's no reason to worry. I'll meet Detective Cavanaugh tomorrow morning and answer any questions he has. And then I'll do whatever I can to help him figure out what happened to her."

"About that. I'm hoping to set up hidden cameras in your store."

"Oh." There was a slight pause. "I can ask Melissa to let you in when the store reopens. But I have cameras already set up inside. Is there a reason you think I need more?"

"First, I'd like it kept between you and me, if possible."

"I can trust Melissa," she insisted.

"Until we figure out what happened to Kelsie, I think it's best to keep it a secret."

"I don't like this," Georgia said.

"It's for the best. As soon as we clear Melissa, we can let her in on what we're doing." I didn't like it either, but I recently had to put a good friend of mine away, so I was much less trusting than I used to be. "I know it's hard to keep secrets from people you care about, but it's necessary. Just for a little while."

"All right," she relented. "As soon as they let me reopen the store, I'll let you know. How many cameras?"

"I have four. They won't be hooked up to your internet, so no one will be able to discover them if they looked. I know you have cameras already set up, but I'm concerned someone tampered with your footage."

The silence was longer this time. "All over books?" she said.

"Expensive books," I added. "And they might be looking for additional ones to steal."

"Well, I called you in for a reason. Though I have to admit you seem very good at investigating. Are you moonlighting as a PI or something?" She laughed, but it trailed off when I didn't reciprocate. "Oh. Are you?"

"I've been involved in a few cases back in Silverwood, so you aren't too far off. I'm thinking about getting a PI license, but I'm not an official investigator. Yet."

I could almost hear Georgia's surprise over the phone. "Then I guess I called in the right person," she said, her voice full of bemusement.

"Let's hope. I'll let you go. If I find anything out before you hear about the store, I'll call you."

"Sounds good."

"Take care, Georgia. Try to get some rest tonight."

"Thanks. Same to you."

We hung up just in time for me to pull into my driveway. Glad to be home, I hurried into the house, kicking my shoes off before I'd shut the front door behind me.

The sweater came next, and I tossed it onto my bed before changing into joggers and a tank top. Thick socks came next, and I put a new cardigan on. Once I tied my hair up, I took a look in the mirror, grimacing at the dark circles under my eyes.

I had to get to bed early tonight. Weeks of stress were wearing on me. Sighing, I went to the kitchen and rummaged through the fridge for something easy to eat for dinner.

When nothing jumped out at me, I got a loaf of bread out of the pantry. Comfort food was calling my name.

Grilled cheese coming right up.

The next morning, I woke up to Poppy on my chest yowling her displeasure.

"Hey," I croaked. "You okay?"

She lifted her tail and plopped onto her butt. One ear twitched and she yowled again. When she did this, I knew to listen.

"All right. I'm up. What is it?"

Poppy hopped off the bed, stopped and looked back at

me to ensure I was getting up, and lifted her tail before hurrying out of the bedroom.

I groaned and reached for the cotton robe hanging on the chair by the nightstand. Tying it around me, I slid my feet into slippers and followed my ornery cat.

Poppy had jumped onto the table next to my laptop.

"I need coffee first," I muttered, giving Poppy the evil eye.

She sneezed, her tail swishing back and forth as she stared at me.

For some odd reason, my laptop was open. I thought I'd closed it last time I used it, but not only was it open, someone had accessed the internet browser.

Maybe not someone. I cast an odd glance at the cat. Perhaps *something?*

Frowning at Poppy, I poured myself a cup of coffee, thankful I remembered to set the timer to start brewing at six a.m. It wasn't even halfway finished, but I'd bought the one that had the automatic shut off if you moved the pot out of the way.

I was the kind of person who almost always moved the pot to fill my mug before the brew finished. The world could not wait for me to be properly caffeinated.

Once the brew was made, and I sat at the table with the open laptop, I scratched Poppy behind the ears and leaned forward.

The page was open to a site called *Ambergris Antiquities*. I wasn't sure what I was looking at, so I clicked around on the site. I was about to close the browser when I spotted something that made me sit up straighter.

Rare Books.

I glanced at Poppy who still sat next to the laptop grooming herself. "You found this?"

She stopped and glanced at me with those strange yellow-green eyes.

I snorted. "'Course you did." The site didn't tell me much, but it did list some books they had for sale and current things they were looking for. I scrolled down that list and paused when I noticed The Birds of America. Odd to see that twice in such a short time.

Once I marked the site on my bookmark area, I was about to close it down when Poppy yowled again. I jerked my hand away and looked at her. She stopped abruptly and stared.

Shaking my head at her antics, I started to close it again, only for this demon to yowl again.

"Poppy! What in the world?"

She came closer and batted at my hand.

"Did I miss something?"

Poppy stared at me with that intense look that always made me nervous.

"Darn cat," I muttered. With a sigh, I investigated the website further, waiting for an aha moment to jump out at me. After a few minutes of searching, I was still no closer to finding out what Poppy wanted me to see than I was when I first started.

I looked at her. "Where is it?"

Poppy tilted her head. "Mreeooooowwr?"

"Sure." Shaking my head, I clicked on the About Us page.

Poppy went completely still. I glanced at her, then back to the page, and scrolled down until my fingers froze in mid-scroll.

Three bios were listed on the page, one of them with a picture of Kelsie Smith. But the name listed there wasn't Kelsie.

It was Alice Montgomery. "Oh, Poppy. You clever little feline." I reached over and scratched underneath her chin. She meowed at me, submitted to my ministrations for a moment, before jumping down and padding back to the bedroom for another nap.

I watched her with amusement until she rounded the corner, then turned my attention back to Alice's bio. She was young, pretty, and not from this area. Alice Montgomery was from the west coast, California to be exact. She'd gone to a state school before training in antiques.

Her specialty was rare books.

I blew out a breath and sat back sipping my coffee as I thought. What was she doing all the way across the country?

People moved all the time, but Kelsie had come to work for Georgia under false pretenses. Page Turner's didn't specialize in rare books. She had a few, but her store wasn't like mine. Was Kelsie working with someone to find something that this antiquities place wanted? Or was I reading too much into this? Kelsie might have been running from a dangerous ex, or maybe she witnessed a crime. My mind spun with all the possibilities.

Then again, sometimes the easiest explanation was the right one.

It was too early to call Georgia, and I had to open the store today anyway. I'd text her during a lull in business later on.

NINE

Cole leaned against my store's brick facade. He straightened when he saw my Rav 4 pull up and waved. Curious, but not alarmed, I greeted him when I got out of the car. The construction crew should arrive in a couple of hours, but for now everything was quiet.

"Hey, Dakota!"

"Morning, Cole. Everything okay?"

He handed me a steaming cup of coffee. "For you."

"Oooh! I love these kinds of visits." I took a sip of the coffee. "Lavender vanilla? You have a good memory."

Cole shrugged. "You going inside?"

"Sure am. Coming in for a bit?"

He nodded. "Just for a few. I know you need to open."

Cole helped me with my bag and keys, and when we were inside, he plopped down onto the couches by the window. He was dressed casually this morning in a pair of dark wash jeans and a blue Henley with a pair of sunglasses sitting on top of his mussed blond hair.

I busied myself with opening duties. Cole would speak when he was ready.

In the meantime, I had an amazing, flavored coffee to enjoy while he pondered.

It took him almost fifteen minutes before he spoke. Cole didn't come into the bookstore too often, but I noticed when he did, he seemed to relax more than I'd ever seen him.

"I heard a story about a death in Copper Canyon," he began.

I groaned. "Is my name tied up in it?"

Cole laughed. "No. I mean, *I* know you're involved, but no one else does. Hardy did a good job at keeping you shielded." He winked at me. "It wasn't a big leap to connect the dots once I realized it was at a bookstore."

"What do you need from me?"

Cole grinned. "I noticed the victim's name is Kelsie Smith."

"It is," I agreed. "I found her yesterday evening."

"Murder?" Cole asked, his eyes alight with the thrill of the hunt.

"Cole," I said with a warning tone.

"The story will be on the front page of every bordering town, Dakota. This is your chance to make sure it's accurate."

I stared at him. "And how does Hardy feel about that?"

He rolled his eyes. "When have I ever cared how Hardy feels?"

"Cole!" I laughed in surprise. Sometimes they got along. Sometimes they acted like mortal enemies. It had to be difficult to be a law enforcement officer and deal with people like Cole who might endanger your case if you let the wrong information slip. Plus, Hardy wasn't very relaxed about anything. I saw his stern demeanor slip a few times, but it was only in our most private moments.

I settled in the chair opposite him, still holding the latte he bought me. "I can't tell you much. I only saw her body. There was nothing about it that seemed violent." There was no blood and no wound I could see.

Cole frowned. "What time did you find her?"

"Around six, I think. Right before the store closed."

I had no plans to tell him I discovered who Kelsie was. If Cole didn't ask the question, I wasn't planning on bringing it up.

"Does Georgia know about Kelsie's false identity?"

I nodded. "But it wasn't until after I found Kelsie's body. Georgia was stacked with customers when I came in, so I browsed through the store while she was busy."

He wrote something down in his notebook. "Did you see anyone or anything suspicious?"

I laughed. "It's a bookstore, Cole. Shady people normally don't come in browsing for books on how to commit crimes."

Cole's lips turned up. "Hilarious," he said dryly. "No

one was acting strange? Glancing toward the section? Hurrying out without buying anything?"

"Nope. I saw nothing alarming until I stumbled over Kelsie."

He gave me a piercing look like he knew I was hiding something but couldn't figure out what it was. "Nothing at all?"

"Not at all." His look made me snort. "You know me well enough to know if I don't want to tell you information, I'll say that. There was absolutely nothing suspicious about that day."

"Hmm. Any other info you haven't shared?"

That question made me chuckle. "Nope. Too broad. Narrow your question, and I'll see if I can share."

When his head jerked up, I grinned and stood. "Gotta get to work. The crew will be here in a little while, and I need to be mentally prepared for the noise."

"Dakota!"

"Isn't digging for the truth part of the thrill of your job?" I asked.

Cole's mouth fell open. "Fine," he growled, packing up his stuff.

"Thanks for the coffee."

He shook his head, but I saw the amusement in his eyes when he stood. "Come here, you heathen." He held his arms out, and I stepped into them for a hug.

"See you later, Cole."

"See you." He stepped back, adjusting the strap of his

briefcase, and headed out the door once I unlocked it for him.

Still smiling, I locked up and headed back to the register to finish up.

Halfway through the day, I had to take an ibuprofen to tamp down the headache swirling behind my eyes. Bookstores had a reputation for being quiet, but the construction crew blew that right out the window with all the hammering and sawing.

But things took an interesting turn after lunch.

I'd just gotten back into my car after grabbing a sandwich at the local deli when my phone went off with a text.

Come back ASAP. Something you need to see.

I blinked at my phone. The text came from Mitchell. He never sent messages like this, so something was definitely up.

Something that would more than likely cost me a lot of money. Sighing, I juggled my drink and bag, fumbling with the car keys. Once I was situated, I hurried back, hoping Mitchell was just being overdramatic.

The foreman was waiting for me at the register when I returned, a strange expression on his face. I breezed in, set everything down, and wiped my clammy hands down the front of my pants. I was nervous and had no idea why.

"Everything okay?"

He jerked his head in the direction of the expansion. "You want to eat first?"

"Will it take long?" I asked.

"Nah. Not to see it. Maybe to figure out what you want to do about it, but not to take a look."

My brows lifted. "Err. Okay. I'll take a look now, I guess."

Mitchell laughed at my expression. "Don't worry, Miss Dakota. We didn't find a body or anything."

I snorted. The foreman was local to Silverwood and familiar with all my exploits.

"Funny," I muttered.

Mitchell led me toward the back of the expansion to the area where he was supposed to knock out a wall earlier. He stopped in front of it, and I gawked at how much more open the space looked now.

"We knocked this out like you wanted but got more than we bargained for when we did." He held out his hand for me.

I glanced down at it and back up at him. Shrugging, I took it. Mitchell never touched me, so this was new, but there must be a lot of debris around.

"Careful," he said as he led me inside. "Step where I step."

I did as he asked, Mitchell carefully navigating me through fallen wood and concrete.

I expected to see a hole in the wall. Or mold. Or anything except what stood in front of me. A brand-new room (to me, at least) with shiny, original hardwood floors, exposed wooden beams, and a massive antique safe with a rusted handle and strange combination lock.

"Whoa," I murmured.

"Yes, ma'am," Mitchell agreed. "We stopped work right away. If it were me, I'd keep most of this room the same. The craftsmanship is beautiful. However, I'd close this back up and make this a room you use for an office. Opening this place to the public will end in damage, especially by kids."

His tone was so dry it told me he had personal experience with children damaging things. I tamped down my smile and stepped further into the room. "This floor is original?"

Mitchell nodded as he walked beside me. He'd let go of my hand now that we were past the worst of it. "Difficult to replace, so I wouldn't change a thing. The wooden beams are original as well. I'd love to know who built the original structure."

I bent down and peered closer at the safe.

"I don't know much about safes, but I expect that one came sometime in the 1900s. You have quite an incredible find here. I did the work here myself and kept my crew away, but at least one of them saw it."

I peered up at him. "You think I should stop work?"

Mitchell shrugged. "We got the other door in and have the lock set up. All my employees are under strict NDAs never to disclose anything they find in the places they work, but you never know. It's possible there's nothing in that safe, but I wouldn't bet on it."

"All right. How about you take the next few days off until I can get this opened?"

He nodded. "Yes ma'am. But you know I'll—"

"Have to charge me?" I lifted a brow in amusement. "I wouldn't dream of it any other way."

Mitchell grinned. "My brother is a locksmith. No idea if he can help, but I can call him if you'd like. He lives here and has a small shop down the road. He works on modern stuff mostly, but he's a geek when it comes to security."

"I'd love that, Mitchell. Can you see if he can come by today?"

Mitchell chuckled. "I bet he'll be here in the next half hour."

He held his hand out. "Let me help you out before we shut it down for the day."

I rose and allowed him to lead me back into the expansion area. Without asking, Mitchell sealed up the area with plastic tarping and tape, barking at his men to pack it up for the day due to a "structural" issue.

He winked at me as he said it.

I'd dealt with a few contractors in my time and had to admit, Mitch might be my favorite.

TEN

Mitchell's brother was devilishly handsome and quick-witted. He had the same lanky build as his brother, but he was a couple inches shorter and quicker to smile.

"Rocco," he said and stuck his hand out to shake.

"Dakota. Want to come on back?"

Rocco glanced around the bookstore, his sharp gaze taking everything in, before nodding and following me to the back. I closed half an hour early today so I could squeeze him in. He had another appointment once he left here, and I was dying to know what was in the safe.

He stopped at the entrance to the extra room and put his hand out. "Mitch wouldn't have left it like this if it wasn't structurally sound, but there are still a lot of things to trip over. Mind if I go first?"

"Not at all."

Rocco stepped over a few things, then did the same as

Mitch had and held out his hand for me to take. Two gentlemen in one family. Their mom must be a good one.

Like Mitch's hand, his was rough and warm. I allowed him to guide me over until once again, we stood in front of the antique safe.

He whistled long and low. "I've never had the pleasure of seeing a safe this old." Rocco bent down and ran his hands over the front and sides of it. He tested the handle and messed with the lock before getting up and trying to see the back. It wasn't pushed all the way against the wall, but it was close enough that he couldn't move it.

"You aren't planning to move this, I hope?" He glanced back at me.

"Uh. No. I assume that weighs at least 500 pounds?"

Rocco chuckled. "No ma'am. I'd guess at least 2,000."

I blinked at him. "Seriously?"

"You must have a well-built foundation to sustain all that weight. Mitch said he knocked the wall down and it was just sitting here?"

"Sure was." I shook my head. "All this time and I never once guessed I had a secret like this hiding in the shop."

Rocco chuckled. "The woodwork and brick in here are fantastic, but the best part might be whatever is waiting in that safe."

I had no idea the building was even that old. It seemed more feasible that someone built around it, but why would they cover it up? Had the person I bought the shop from known about it? If so, why didn't he take it with him when he left?

I had way more questions than answers.

"Can you open it?" I asked.

He tucked his thumbs in his belt loops. "Yes, ma'am. It's going to take a while, but I can do it."

"How much is it going to cost me?"

Rocco sent me a side-eye. "You friends with my brother?"

I wanted to say yes for a potential discount, but I wouldn't jeopardize my relationship with Mitch for ten percent off a service. "He's my contractor. I like him, but we haven't moved to friendship yet."

"I see. He likes working here, and I've never been able to crack a safe this old. You free tomorrow evening after six?"

"For safe cracking? Absolutely."

Rocco laughed. "Good. If you order dinner, I'll do it for free."

I stilled. "Seriously?"

He patted his stomach. "Man's gotta eat, don't he? I don't have a wife or a girlfriend, and our mom has passed on. I can't cook worth a lick, so dinnertime is always questionable."

"That's all you want?" I asked suspiciously.

"That's it. Even if it's pizza. I'm not picky."

I didn't get a bad feeling about Rocco. It was the opposite, in fact. He seemed like a decent guy, and he was related to Mitch. This was a small town, and he'd been here for years.

"You like pasta?" I asked.

"I like anything," he answered.

"Fair enough. Pasta it is. Tomorrow at six thirty?"

"You got yourself a deal, Dakota." He held out his hand and led me back through the debris. "I'll get Mitch out before then and have him get some of this stuff out of the way if that's okay."

"Fine by me."

When we were out, he let go and hitched his bag higher on his shoulder. "I'll see you tomorrow then. In the meantime, I wouldn't breathe a word about this to anyone." He frowned. "Silverwood has great people, but not everyone is reliable. The mystery of it might bring out some ne'er do wells."

"Will do." I thought the same thing myself.

Rocco headed to the door. "I'll keep this to myself and meet you here tomorrow." His dark eyes sparkled. "I can't wait to crack that thing open. It's been ages since I've had a true locksmith challenge."

I let out a surprised laugh. It appeared I'd met my first locksmithing nerd. "See you then." I opened the door for him and waved once he stepped out.

What was in that safe? Thoughts of Georgia came to the forefront of my mind. The portion of the wall knocked out was partially on my side, and partially on the new property, though the safe was sitting on mine. What would have happened if someone had discovered this before me and owned the other part of the building?

Life was funny that way sometimes. Either way, I had to be careful to keep this to myself to avoid any long-lost relatives from coming out of the woodwork to see if anything valuable surfaced from the safe.

I did a last sweep of the store, taking care of a few things I'd forgotten to do during the day, before I shut off the lights and headed home.

Poppy curled around my feet while I stood at the stove stirring spaghetti sauce. It was my Gran's recipe, and one that was always a hit at parties. Not that I went to many parties, but Gran was quite the social butterfly these days. The scent of bay leaves and Italian seasonings filled the house with a gorgeous, herbal fragrance.

I didn't often make spaghetti these days because it was only me, but since I had a locksmith who was doing me a huge favor in exchange for dinner, I'd put on a huge pot. Tomorrow, I'd pack it up and bring a crockpot for later. There was a small stove in the back of the store I could make fresh noodles at. I'd save some for me to eat the next couple of days and pack the rest up for Rocco.

As I cooked, I chatted away to Poppy who said nothing but continued twining around my legs. I told her about the safe and my hopes it would have old gold coins from the Wild West, and I'd be able to retire to Tahiti.

Not really. I was happy here, and the bookstore was all I ever wanted, but a nice long vacation on a beach wouldn't be amiss.

When the sauce reached a boil, I turned the heat down to a low simmer and put the lid back on.

Two and a half hours, and dinner would be ready.

I reached down and picked Poppy up, dropping a

couple of kisses on her sweet little face and giving her a nuzzle as I walked into the living room. "You are a good kitty," I murmured against her fur. She nuzzled my face, then squirmed out of my grip.

"No more snuggles for me?"

She meowed and took off.

That was a resounding no.

I sat on the couch and poured myself a glass of wine before curling my feet under me and flipping the television on.

Being single meant never having to share the remote control.

ELEVEN

Harper waved at me on her way out that evening. "Got a date!" she called, grinning at me as she jogged down the steps.

"Have fun!"

"Seafood night!" she said with a laugh. "Can't wait!"

I shook my head, smiling as I locked up behind her. Rocco would be here in forty-five minutes, and I had spaghetti sauce to heat up and pasta to cook. The sauce would taste even better today.

A knock on the door roused me out of my spaghetti reverie. I tapped the spoon on the side of the crockpot and set it on top of a paper plate. The pasta still had a few minutes to go. I wiped my hands on a clean towel and hurried to the front to open the door.

Rocco stood there, the same leather bag tossed over his shoulders. I opened the door and gestured him in, freezing when I saw a familiar, unmarked car cruising down the road. Hardy and I locked eyes. His attention flicked from me to Rocco, expression darkening when he saw the man entering the store.

My heart lurched sideways, but I couldn't help whatever conclusion he decided to come to. I didn't bother to wave, instead stepping inside and closing the door behind us.

Rocco noticed my face. "Dakota?" He stepped forward in concern. "Are you okay?"

I let out the breath I'd been holding and shook my head. "No." My voice came out a croak. "Yes. Fine. I'm fine."

His brow furrowed. "You sure?"

Pushing away from the door, I led him to the back. "Dinner will be finished in just a minute."

Rocco followed me. "Finished?"

"Get ready to try the best spaghetti in Silverwood Hollow," I said boldly, grinning at him as I picked up the spoon.

He peered over my shoulder at the bubbling sauce. "That smells divine," he said. "Anything I can do to help?"

I pointed the spoon at the spaghetti noodles. "There's a colander in the sink. Mind draining those?"

"For a homecooked meal? Anything."

While Rocco did that, I turned the crockpot to warm and took the parmesan out of the fridge.

A few minutes later, I handed Rocco an enormous bowl of spaghetti and a slice of garlic bread—not homemade. I was a good cook, but bread making was an entirely different ballgame.

Rocco stared at it like I'd handed him a pile of diamonds.

"Come on," I said gently, touching him on the forearm. "There's a place to sit out front."

I took my bowl and a bottle of red wine and led Rocco to the seating area.

He immediately dug in and groaned when he finished the first bite. "Mitch didn't tell me you were an amazing cook."

I shrugged. "I've never made him a meal. Just the occasional cookie. He didn't tell you?"

Rocco laughed. "And give up his cookie dealer? Never."

We grinned at each other. "The rest of the sauce in the crockpot is for you. I think it should last you at least three days."

His fork paused in midair. "For me?"

"It's the least I can do."

Rocco nodded. "Dakota, I think this is the start of a beautiful friendship."

It took Rocco two hours and another plate of spaghetti to crack the combination. When I heard that glorious click, I threw my fist up in the air and let out a shout.

Rocco's delighted smile was something to behold. He winced as he stood, rubbing his knees with a grimace. "I'll step outside and let you take the first peek, Dakota." He pulled a notebook from his back pocket and jotted down the combination. "Here's what it is now, but I recommend you change it tonight. I'll show you how before I leave."

"Thanks, Rocco."

He smiled and carefully made his way out.

My heartbeat turned thunderous, and I didn't know why. The odds of something being left behind were low, but if it was empty, why was it locked?

I stood there for at least a minute, my thoughts racing.

Just get it over with, I told myself.

My knees popped when I settled myself on the ground. Holding my breath, I reached for the handle.

TWELVE

A leather ledger lay on top. I pulled it out and flipped through the pages. Spidery handwriting with hundreds of numbers was the only thing on the page.

Other documents lay underneath.

Several oversized diamond shaped envelopes lay underneath those. My heart lay in my throat. I sat here flipping through history.

With gentle hands, I removed the first. It felt heavy but flexible. Documents or other paperwork lay inside. Maybe an unbound book.

The thought of it being a book brought a smile to my face. It had to be at least a hundred years old. My fingers trembled as I slid the envelope open, revealing a large sheath of papers with colorful illustrations.

Birds.

"Oh my goodness," I whispered. My trembling fingers turned into a full-on shake. I put the envelope back into the safe, rose, and hurried back into the bookshop for a pair of gloves.

Rocco stayed in the seating area, flipping through a magazine from the table. When he heard me, he lowered it. "Finished already?"

I held up a finger. "Need gloves."

Rocco's brows lifted. He watched as I rummaged through one of the drawers by the register until I found a pair of soft cotton gloves. I waved them at him and hurried back into the room.

Rocco merely watched, his lips tilted in amusement.

Skidding to a stop in front of the steps, I hit my knees and reached in for the envelope. If this was what I thought it was…

I let out a breath.

No. It couldn't be.

I brought the sheath out again and stood, setting it on top of the safe. I slowly flipped through each illustration, emotion welling to the surface. Every picture was meticulously drawn and painted with what I thought might be watercolor. I knew next to nothing about birds, so the only one I was able to identify was a turkey. When I finished with that sheath, I carefully replaced it and went through the next.

An hour later, I replaced everything but left the door open so Rocco could show me how to change the combination.

I called him back and smiled, but my expression must have looked strange.

"Everything okay?" he asked.

"Yes. Just books."

"Oh. So that's good, right?"

Several million dollars good, I thought. "Yes. Great. I've never found a bad book."

My awkward laugh didn't sound convincing, but Rocco just gave me an odd look and knelt by the safe.

"Ready to change the combination?" he asked.

"Yes, please."

He patted the space beside him. "I'll run through it until you fully understand. I'll have you change it once while I'm here, then you can change it again once I leave. Sound good?"

I nodded, the blood still roaring through my veins. I'd potentially found the treasure of a lifetime.

But as I flipped through the pages a little while before, I also wondered if I'd also found a motive for murder.

Rocco left some time later, once he was confident I knew how to change the combinations. I headed straight back to the safe and changed it to something I fully committed to memory. Writing it down might be a disaster if I lost it somewhere in the fathomless depths of my purse.

Once I was satisfied I'd gotten it right, I shut the safe door and slumped to the floor. A thought had been circling around in my head since I realized what I might have. Keeping what was in the safe *safe* was my top priority.

And the only way I knew how to do it was to speak to the one person I didn't want to speak to at all.

I sat there for a while staring at the ceiling until I felt

brave enough to get my cell out and hit the first number on my important contacts list.

Hardy answered on the first ring.

"I'm surprised to hear from you," he said, his voice a quiet rumble in my ear.

"Can you come by the shop?" I said without preamble. "It's important."

"Are you hurt?" I could almost feel Hardy snapping to attention.

"No. I'm not. I—there's something here I need help with, though, and I don't think there's anyone else I can ask."

"I'll be there in less than ten minutes. Don't leave the shop."

"I wasn't planning on it."

The line went dead. A sigh escaped me as I buried my face in my hands.

Hardy still had a key to the shop and let himself in. I knew I should get it back, but I didn't have the heart to do it. Plus, he was a detective. Was there any person worthier of having a key than someone like Hardy?

"Dakota!" he barked.

"In the expansion area!" I called.

Hardy's boots thumped through the building until I heard him step into the new area. "Dakota?" he said, quieter this time.

"Back behind the plastic tarp. Be careful. There's a lot of debris around. Mitch couldn't make it tonight to clear it out of the way."

"Are you sure you're okay?" he asked again, his voice vibrating with concern.

"I promise I'm okay. I just—Hardy, can you just come back, please?"

He didn't say anything, but his footsteps picked up. The tarp rustled, revealing Hardy's dark head. His sharp-eyed gaze swept the room, unrelenting until it landed on me.

My heart skipped a beat when I saw the relief on his face once he spotted me. I offered a weak smile. "Hi."

His brow wrinkled. "Hi."

I patted the safe. "Mitch took down the wall today and found this behind it."

Hardy came closer and crouched in front of it, running his hand over the surface. "This is old. More than a hundred years." He shook his head. "I don't understand. Is this why you called me?" Hardy huffed a laugh. "If you're worried about someone stealing it, I wouldn't be. Someone is going to need a truck and multiple people to move this. Even then, it wouldn't happen in a hurry."

"I'm not worried about the safe."

He lifted his eyes to meet mine. Understanding dawned in them. "What's in it?"

"I suspect it's an original book worth several million dollars."

Hardy rarely showed emotion. This time, he reared back on his heels, his eyes widening almost comically. He blew out a slow breath. "Dakota."

"I know," I whispered. "I think this might have something to do with Kelsie Smith's death."

He nodded. "The thief is looking for something. You think it's this."

"It has to be. Georgia gave me a list of missing books. Several of them were about birds."

Hardy's brow wrinkled. "Birds? You have a book worth millions and it's about birds?"

He read here and there, but, like me, he didn't know squat about birds. I handed him my gloves. "Put these on."

Hardy did as I asked while I opened the safe one more time. Hardy peered into it and whistled low. "All of those envelopes?"

I pulled the top one out. "Here. Be very careful handling the pages."

Hardy treated the work with the reverence it deserved, careful not to wrinkle any pages. He flipped through each, studying the drawings one by one. When he finished, he slid them back into the envelope and handed it back to me.

"Does that say Audubon?" he asked quietly.

I nodded.

He scrubbed a hand over his face. "Dakota."

Hardy said my name a lot when he was disturbed.

"I don't know what to do," I admitted.

Hardy sank back down to the floor. I followed. We sat across from each other staring at the safe.

"You have cameras in the shop?"

I nodded. "Not in the expansion part, but I can move a few over here."

"I'd start there."

"Okay." I started to stand, but Hardy got there first and held a hand out to help me up. I hesitated for a moment before sliding my hand into his.

His touch made me tear up. I kept my head down to keep him from noticing. Hardy didn't let go until we were back in the main area of the store.

"Who knows?" he asked.

"My contractor, maybe a couple of his guys, and the locksmith who came by earlier."

His eyes flashed with relief when I mentioned the locksmith, but I didn't acknowledge it.

"Too many people," he said after a long moment. He let out a heavy breath. "I'm inclined to have the safe moved tonight."

"Where?"

"Police station," he said.

My eyes narrowed. "I'm not inclined to have my property seized by the police," I said sternly.

Hardy's lips tugged into a smile. "I'm not seizing anything. I'm commandeering something for your own safety."

"And taking it to the police station where I might encounter trouble getting it back, and more people than ever will be in my business."

He stepped forward and put both hands on top of my shoulders. "Dakota."

I rolled my eyes. "Hardy."

"I'm going to put it in my office. That's all. Just for safekeeping. You can have it back once we find Georgia's thief."

It was a good offer. Hardy would keep it safe, and someone would have to be a fool to break into the police station, especially a detective's office. But bringing it in might open him up to a lot of questions from curious people.

I couldn't move the safe on my own, but taking the volumes out and bringing them home would open them up to not only theft, but damage too.

The former owner of Tattered Pages had passed a while ago, and I didn't dare contact his family in case it opened me up to litigation.

My mother had ensured the contract I signed for this place had a clause in it stating I was entitled to all the contents left behind whether known or unknown, and I'd done the same for the bookstore. Mom called it an assumption clause, but I don't think that's what it's called. Whatever was in that safe was mine, but it wouldn't stop someone from filing a lawsuit anyway.

Greed drove people to do a lot of things they normally wouldn't.

I trusted Hardy to do the right thing. I trusted him even more to do right by me. Things might be weird between us now, but I still cared about him, and from the way he looked at me, he still cared about me, too.

"Fine," I relented. "You think you can move it tonight?"

"I do. We'll set up a barrier so no one will see what we're moving out."

"That's a good idea." I slumped. "Thanks, Hardy."

"Any time." He pulled his cell out and called someone, turning away when they answered. Hardy spoke in a low voice, pacing the floor as they talked. When he hung up, he turned to me. "I have a few trustworthy guys coming over in about fifteen minutes. They'll bring a pickup and a hand truck. Not sure it will be enough, but we'll make do."

"Should I stick around?" It was pitch dark outside, and I was exhausted.

Hardy shrugged. "Up to you, but there's no reason you need to. I'll lock up when we finish." He gave me a gentle smile. "Go home and get some rest."

I looked up at his handsome face. "I really appreciate this."

"Anything for you." He touched my chin with his thumb. Time stretched between us, our breaths the only sound in the room. It took everything I had to step away.

Hardy's eyes flickered. He gave me a short nod. "Be careful going home. I'll text you when it's finished."

I waved and grabbed my sweater and purse, feeling better now that I'd left things in Hardy's hands. If it were anyone else, I wouldn't have left. Millions of dollars lay in that safe. The only one I trusted with it was Hardy.

I didn't have the heart to investigate that thought any further tonight.

THIRTEEN

Harper was off today. Thank goodness because I didn't want to drag her into any danger. Or any more than I already had. Hardy had texted me late last night with two simple words.

Package secured.

I fell asleep only a few minutes after receiving it, secure in the knowledge that Hardy was keeping it safe.

Mitch showed up around nine with a skeleton crew. I'd never taken the time to meet many of his workers, because I was usually busy or they were, so we became ships passing in the night. This morning was a little different. The store wasn't open yet, and I'd caught up on all the extra work I had before Rocco had arrived.

I greeted each person, offering them fresh coffee. Each one of them accepted, introducing themselves as I handed each a cup. Two resembled each other enough to be broth-ers. One was darker skinned with an accent I couldn't place. He didn't speak much English, but his smile was beautiful, and sometimes a smile was a universal language.

The last person was a taller man who wouldn't meet my eyes. He accepted a disposable cup with a muttered thank you and turned away, walking over to a work bench. He had blond hair and watery blue eyes, a weak chin, and poor posture. The man didn't look like he belonged on a construction crew, but who was I to judge someone's skill based on their physical appearance?

Brushing off my uncharitable thoughts, I offered the last cup to Mitch and murmured a quiet thanks.

"No need. Rocco shared that amazing spaghetti sauce with me. My grandmother would have wept with envy if she were still alive."

"I'll have to tell Gran," I said, beaming with pride. "She's been serving that recipe my entire life."

"Please extend my sincerest thanks to her as well." He jerked his head toward the torn down wall. "I don't see the safe. I hope you planned it like that."

I laughed. "I did. I plan on contacting the historical society later to examine some of the ledgers."

"You never know. It might be worth something."

"Or I could use it as a conversation starter in the store."

Mitchell shrugged. "Can't say I know much about books, but I think I'd rather have the money." He winked, his eyes sparkling with amusement. "We'll get out of your hair now, Dakota. Let us know if you need anything. Today we hope to have the new doors dividing the shop hung. We'll keep those closed to cut down on the noise."

"That sounds wonderful." I raised my coffee cup to him. "I'll be in the shop all day. Give me a shout if you need something."

I left the workers there and headed back into the book-store area to start the day.

The shop bustled with customers for most of the day, the only lull around lunchtime. Mitch and his staff had vacated for a bite to eat, leaving me in the quiet shop. I let out a long sigh of relief and pulled my cellphone out to call for a sandwich delivery. The local deli had a meatball sub that was calling my name.

After lunch, my phone rang. Georgia's name flashed on the screen, so I answered, tossing the empty sandwich wrapper in the trash.

"The police have cleared the area," she said. "Melissa isn't due in until tomorrow. Can you come by tonight with the cameras?"

I had an empty schedule, so I agreed. We chatted a little more and hung up. Relief filled me at her upbeat tone. Georgia seemed to be doing much better than she had been when I last saw her. Finding a body would shake anyone up. Even after all this time, I hadn't hardened myself to it, and I hoped I never would. Every person belonged to someone—even if they weren't likable.

A few more workers wandered in after lunch, one a shorter man with a receding hairline and crooked teeth, but lively blue eyes, and the other, taller, handsome, and leanly muscled. Both nodded to me as they headed into the expansion area, and I made a mental note to remind Mitch to tell his people to use the other door now that it was installed.

It wasn't that I minded them accessing it, but it sometimes threw customers off to see construction workers coming in and out. They thought the store wasn't open and that was the last thing I needed with all the changes in my life over the last few weeks.

I had balloons outside with a pretty chalk sign saying I was open, but all the trucks and tarping everywhere made it look like the sign was old. Pretty soon I'd have to stand outside with a megaphone and wave people in. I couldn't wait until this was over and things were back to normal.

A few hours later, Mitch poked his head through the extra door. "We're heading out. Need anything else?"

"Nope. Have a good evening." I waved and grabbed my purse from the hook. "I'm right behind you."

PAGE TURNER'S looked no worse for the wear. The police tape was gone, but the lights on the store were still out. Georgia's car was parked in the reserved spot. I whipped my SUV in next to her vehicle and headed up to the door.

She answered on the first knock. "Hey, Dakota." Georgia waved me in. "I had a cleaning company come in earlier." Dark circles had made a home under her eyes. "Everything looks the way it did before." She rubbed her mouth. "Even though I can't stop seeing her lying there."

I reached over and squeezed her hand. "I'm so sorry.

Don't feel rushed to reopen the store." It was just me and Harper at Tattered Pages, but I could probably spare some time. "If you want, I can come in and help out a couple days this week if you need some more time."

Georgia blinked in surprise. "You'd do that for me?"

"Why wouldn't I? Just let me know, and I'll move some things around on my calendar."

She smiled. "I really appreciate it. It's not necessary, but it's so kind of you to offer." Georgia stood and pointed to the coffee area. "There's fresh water for tea and a fresh pot of coffee set up for you. I'm not sure how long it will take you to set everything up, but you're welcome to help yourself."

"Hopefully not more than half an hour," I said, patting my bag.

She nodded and headed to the back. I fixed myself a cup of coffee and dug through my purse for the cameras. They were small and easy to conceal, but I'd have to make sure they were completely hidden from prying, curious eyes. I had to put them up high and angle them to ensure I had the whole area covered.

A moment later, I ventured deeper into the store to find the best place to install them.

FOURTEEN

I wasn't super technical, but the camera setup ended up not being too difficult.

I flipped through each camera to make sure I had a clear image of the coverage area. When I ensured it was working, I poked my head in the back and called for Georgia.

She came out a moment later. "All finished?"

"They're all ready to go. I'll text you the info so you can access them too. If anything happens after six p.m., you'll get an alert on your phone." I sent her a quick text with the info. "The batteries will last for a long time, but if something goes wrong with them, we'll both get an alert about it."

Georgia frowned down at her phone. "I'll get this set up when I get home this evening." She shook her head and sighed. "Sure wish this wasn't necessary."

"Me too," I murmured. "I'll get out of your hair. Thanks for letting my come by."

"No problem. You still don't want me to tell Melissa?"

"You can tell her once we're sure she's in the clear. It's not ideal, but important for now." I adjusted the strap of my bag. "I'm sure she's in the clear, but we can't be too safe right now."

"All right, Dakota. Thanks for coming by."

"You're welcome." I waved and headed out the door, dropping my empty paper cup into the trash on my way out. "I'll call you tomorrow."

The drive home was easy. Traffic was at a minimum, and I took the back roads. An unfamiliar vehicle sat in my driveway when I turned in. Sitting up straighter, I slowed my car down and tried to get a good look before I stopped. Whoever it was still sat in their car.

Nerves fluttered in my stomach. Before I opened the shop, I wouldn't have batted an eye at someone sitting here, but a lot of things had happened since then. I pulled up beside the vehicle and turned to see a dark-haired woman sitting in the driver's seat.

Hardy's...I wasn't quite sure what she was. Ex-fiancée. Maybe current fiancée? No idea. I hadn't asked.

But why was she here? I looked toward the back of her vehicle, but the child was nowhere to be seen.

Squaring my shoulders, I let out a deep breath and got out of my car.

The woman did the same thing. She came around the driver's side toward me. I held my purse so tight my fingers ached. My heart pounded in my chest, and breathing became difficult.

"Hello," I said, surprised when it sounded normal.

"Dakota?" the woman asked.

"Yes."

She was beautiful. Long, perfectly styled dark hair fell around her shoulders. Her makeup looked airbrushed, or her skin was perfect. Probably the second. She had a sharp jawline, a perfect nose, and rosebud lips painted a blush pink. The woman wore a blue pencil skirt, heels, and a white blouse decorated with a mustard yellow pattern.

I, on the other hand, wore my usual uniform of ankle pants, flats, a long tank, and a long cardigan. My hair was tied up in a messy bun, and I'd only worn mascara and a little lip gloss. "How can I help you?"

Her eyes flicked to the door.

There was literally no way on earth I'd invite her in. I'm surprised she thought that was an option.

"I'm Maria."

Of course she had a pretty name, too.

"Hello, Maria."

A smile that looked more like a grimace touched her lips.

I made no move to go inside. "What can I do for you?" I asked again.

"Um." She dropped her gaze. "I know you've seen me before."

I nodded.

"And I'm sure you want to know why I'm here."

"I do."

She snorted. Her fingers twisted around the strap of her purse. "Hardy is still in love with you," she blurted.

I blinked at her and said nothing.

Maria stared at me. "Aren't you surprised by that?"

I tilted my head and studied her. "Well. No. We were in a serious relationship up until a few weeks ago. As you may well know, it takes time to get over something like that."

Maria's jaw tightened. "It's...interfering."

I laughed out loud. The nerve of this woman. "I'm not sure why you're here or what you want from me. This is between you and Hardy. I'm not a part of it." I hitched my bag up higher. "If you'll excuse me." Shaking my head, I clicked the key fob to lock my vehicle and headed up my stairs.

"My daughter deserves better!"

"I'd say so," I muttered, not even concerned with how mean it sounded.

She gasped. "Stay away from him!"

"I haven't been around him unless it was absolutely necessary," I snapped. When I got to the door, I turned. "Get off my property, Maria. Do not come back."

She huffed, her cheeks burning bright red. Maria stood there for a moment more before turning and getting back into her car. I waited on the front porch until her headlights disappeared in the distance.

As soon as I was inside, I pulled out my cellphone and texted Hardy to tell him what happened, without telling him what she said, and asked him to ensure it didn't happen again.

It took Hardy a few minutes to respond, but I saw the three little dots start and stop several times before his message came through.

I'm sorry. It won't happen again.

Nothing else, but it was enough.

I slumped onto the couch and buried my face in my hands.

Solving a murder was fundamentally easier than navigating the treacherous terrain of the human heart.

Sleep was a long time coming, and I felt it when I woke up the next morning. Once I had a large cup of coffee, I settled at the dining table and accessed Georgia's cameras.

Everything looked like it was working well, so I clicked out of the app once I ensured all the cameras were functional. Harper was due to open this morning, so I had most of the day off. I had to stop by to take some inventory, but other than that, I could focus on other things.

First on my list was finding an authenticator. I had a list of several people to call. One of them I knew from college. He wasn't an authenticator back then, just a book lover like me. I hadn't seen him in years, but we occasionally emailed back and forth to check in.

I called him first and got voicemail, so I sent him an email instead asking him if he'd meet in person. Putting the title in an email made me nervous for reasons I couldn't explain, so I told him I might have an incredible find and wanted to speak in person.

The next two people I called also sent the calls to voicemail, so I left messages for them. Both came highly recommended, but I hoped my friend was available. I trusted him way more than I would a stranger.

I realized I'd have to see Hardy again, and that wasn't ideal, but at least the book was safe with him.

One more cup of coffee went down the hatch before I got ready for the day. Just as I was grabbing my purse to head out, my phone rang.

"Harper? Everything okay?"

"I think so." Her voice was lower than usual which concerned me. "We're missing a few books."

I stopped at the front door. "What?"

"I mean, I think we are. I'd need to see the inventory sheets to confirm, and I can't find them."

"I'll be right there." I hung up and hurried out the door.

Apparently, Georgia's problems were at my doorstep now.

The thing is, I had cameras set up all over the store. With a grimace, I remembered Hardy still had access to them as well. I needed to fully extricate everything from him soon, but it was hard to unentangle yourself when you started building a life with someone.

I tamped down the sadness in my heart and hurried to the car. No time to get down in the weeds with my emotions. I had way too much money tied up in the rare books I had in my store and little time to figure out where they'd gone.

Harper was rarely wrong, but I hoped this time she was having an off day.

Mitch and the crew were already there. I tamped down on my suspicions because once that box was opened, I couldn't close it. Being absolutely sure was imperative. I trusted Mitch and wouldn't think he'd do something like this. I also trusted his judgment with his crew, but I didn't know them as well and rarely interacted with them.

I waved, not stopping to talk, and gestured for Harper to follow me to the back.

She nodded and rose, brushing past me to lock the door. I made a beeline for the back office and bent to unlock the file cabinet tucked next to my desk. Once I had the right file, I opened it and pulled out the current inventory.

Harper came in just then and shut the door behind her. She sank into the seat and let out a deep sigh. "I'm so sorry to bother you on your day off, but I thought it was important enough for a call."

"No need to apologize."

She brushed a hand over her bangs to smooth them. There was a furrow between her brows, and a look of stress on her face.

"I think we're missing a Gatsby—"

My hands stilled for a brief second.

Harper noticed it and winced. "Some children's books as well, first printings, but nothing as expensive as the Gatsby." She chewed on the side of her lip. "It's weird.

The children's books I think are missing all have to do with—"

"Birds, right?"

She blinked in surprise. "Uh. Yes. That's exactly right." Harper sat a little straighter. "What's going on?"

I hadn't told Harper anything about Georgia's store. Catching her up, I stopped at the part where I found the body. Harper was great at the bookstore, but I kept her out of a lot of the things I got involved in.

For both of our peace of minds.

She shook her head. "You think he's after something in particular?"

I did not tell her I thought I had an original copy of the bird book our suspect might be looking for. Telling anyone would loop them into what was going on, and I wanted to keep Harper safe.

"I think the thief is hitting up each bookstore in the area trying to find it. I'll need to call Harriet tonight."

Harper nodded. She pulled her sweater closer. "Is that the ledger?" she asked, pointing at the file.

"It is. Want to come with me?"

We rose and headed to the locked cabinet. "Was it locked when you noticed the missing books?"

Harper nodded. "I unlocked it because something about it was bothering me. The order looked different than before."

So someone had a key to my cabinet. Or they were somehow able to open it without it and lock it back. My gaze went to Mitch and his crew. Again, I didn't think

Mitch had anything to do with it. He was the one who pointed out the safe and encouraged me to keep it to myself.

I peered through the glass and frowned. Harper was right. We were missing a few things. Sighing, I unlocked it, then went one by one through the books while Harper checked off the inventory.

It took a little while, but having help sped it along. When we finished, we realized we had five books missing. One was a collector's edition of *The Great Gatsby*, and the others were a mix of children's and nonfiction books where birds had a major focus.

I jotted down all the titles, locked the case, and motioned for Harper to follow me back to the office. "I'm not going to do anything about this for a day or two," I told her.

Harper's brows lifted in surprise, but she didn't argue.

"I'm hoping I'll find Georgia's thief soon. Once I do, I can only hope they'll lead us to all the stolen books. If I have to involve insurance, I will, but I'd prefer to exhaust all avenues to find them first."

"Makes sense," Harper said. "Want me to call a locksmith out?"

"Not yet. I'll take out the ones I can't afford to lose before I leave today, but I'd also like to add something to it."

Harper gave me a curious look. "Which one?"

"The Birds of America."

She whistled low. "You think that's what they're after?"

I nodded. "I have no idea why they think one of us has it. A book like that belongs in a museum. We're all too small time to have an original."

"True," Harper said with a snort. "Though if anyone would have it, I'd put money on you. I've seen some amazing things come into this shop since I've been in here."

Even though I was bursting at the seams, I kept my mouth shut about the safe. If it were authenticated, I'd have to be extremely careful in how I sold it. I'd want to be completely anonymous and ensure every step of the transaction was documented from A to Z. A priceless book like that would bring scammers out of the woodwork.

"I'd be sunning on a yacht in Tahiti if I had one of those," I said dryly. Which, of course, would be one of the first things I did if this thing turned out to be legit.

My cell rang. I answered without looking. "Dakota."

"As I live and breathe," a deep voice said over the line. "It's been ages since I've heard your voice, Dakota."

"Liam?" I smiled at the sound of his voice. "I'm so glad you called!"

"How could I resist that cloak and dagger voice mail?" he drawled. "I'm actually not too far from you. We could meet up this evening if you'd like."

"Really? Where are you?" Liam lived several hours away, one of the many things that prevented us from catching up.

"I have a conference a couple of hours away from Silverwood. We're about to wrap for the day, so it will be a bit of a drive to get to you. Want to say six?"

"Are you sure? I'll buy dinner and a couple tanks of gas and pay your fee, of course."

Liam laughed. "Let's see what we're dealing with first, then we'll talk, but I won't say no to dinner."

"Sounds wonderful." I rattled off the address to the police station and hung up.

Harper stared at me. "You're meeting him at the police station? Should I go with you?"

I waved a hand. "Not at all. It's a little convoluted, but I want Liam to look at something for me. I left it at the police station."

Harper winced. "With Hardy?"

I nodded. "Not ideal, but he's the best person to trust with something like that."

She shook her head. "I suppose. Next time, reach out to me. I'm always happy to help."

"I know that. This was above my pay grade," I admitted. "I needed Hardy's help with it."

Harper rose from her chair. "No problem. I hope he can help you." She glanced at the door. "You don't think..." Her voice trailed off.

"It isn't Mitch," I said adamantly, my voice almost a whisper. "But I can't vouch for some of his workers. It's a good idea to keep the side door shut during the day while they're here." A thought occurred to me.

"Did you check the cameras?"

Harper snapped her fingers. "Oh. Shoot. Yes, I did. I should have told you that first. Nothing." Her brow wrinkled. "I thought it was strange, and then I thought I must have imagined the books being gone. But the camera showed no activity from four thirty on. I didn't notice anything missing when I came in, and I looked inside. The most obvious choice is lunchtime. I left for a sandwich and was gone for maybe forty-five minutes. But the camera doesn't show anyone around it."

It made sense. Either before she came in or when she was out for lunch was the most likely time for a theft. That would put the spotlight on one of Mitch's people. Maybe even more than one if someone had messed with my cameras.

I checked my cellphone for the time. Liam would be here in a couple of hours, and I still had to call Hardy to make sure he could give me access to the safe. The thought of making that phone call sent a spear of dread through my stomach. Seeing Hardy so much had reopened a wound that had finally started to mend. Talking to him wasn't much better.

"Can you hold the fort down? I'm going to speak with Mitch."

Harper nodded. "Should we do that?" She wrung her hands together, her eyes focused on the closed door between the shop and addition. "I don't want there to be an issue with the construction."

"We have to find out." I gave her a hopeful smile. "Mitch is reasonable, and I won't come at it in an accusatory way. I'm going to ask him some questions and see if he's seen anything. He's been great so far, so I think he will take it okay as long as I approach it with care."

Harper blew out a breath. "All right. I guess. I'm just worried about how this is going to go over."

"Having hard conversations is necessary sometimes. Mitch seems like a good guy."

She nodded and stood.

"I'll be right back."

Harper nodded and watched me walk away.

FIFTEEN

Mitch spotted me as soon as I walked in. He held up a hand in a wave, then gestured for me to follow him to the new space where the safe once was.

When I stepped inside, he pulled the plastic tarp back over the space and leaned against one of the support beams. "Everything all right?" he said. "I noticed your assistant acting a little weird today. She keeps glancing over here with a strange look on her face."

"I wish there were chairs," I grumbled. "Tomorrow I'll bring some in."

Mitch crossed his arms over his chest. "Out with it."

A sigh escaped me. "We had some books come up missing."

One of his eyebrows went up. "You think one of my guys did it?" He didn't seem offended, more curious than anything.

"Not necessarily. A friend of mine one town over had

the same kind of theft. We think he's looking for something specific, but the only link between us is the type of store we have." I shrugged. "It's strange to think any of the stores in this area have what we think he's looking for. We're all small-time bookshops. Most of our foot traffic comes from tourism."

"What do you think they're looking for?"

"It's a book by John Audubon."

Mitch straightened. "The Birds of America?"

I blinked. "Yes. You a big reader?"

He laughed. "Nonfiction usually. Though I do enjoy a good thriller here and there. However, I am a big bird watcher. It's sort of a bible in our book club."

I laughed out loud. "You're in a book club?"

Mitch's eyes twinkled. "Just because I'm in construction doesn't mean I'm not an intellectual, Miss Dakota."

"Huh. The things you learn." Shaking my head, I gave Mitch a once-over. He was right. Judging books by their covers was always a mistake, but I did sometimes get taken in by the pretty ones. So did my customers.

But then again, sometimes impulse purchases turned out to be the best purchases.

"Tell me what happened."

"I don't really know. Harper called me and said she thought some things in the locked cabinet came up missing. I came in and accessed the inventory. She's right."

Concern flashed over his face. "You have cameras all over. Did you check them?"

"We did. There's no movement in the shop except for customers."

Mitch shook his head. "That can't be right. Unless—"

"Someone messed with the cameras."

"I'm in construction. Techy stuff isn't my thing."

"Just birds?" I asked with a laugh.

"Just birds," he agreed. "I can ask my guys if you'd like."

"I don't want anyone to think I'm accusing them of something. Just trying to figure it out."

"If anyone of my guys is guilty of this, I need to know about it."

"As do I," I agreed. "How do you want to handle this?"

"If someone is messing with your camera system, then we can't count on that."

I used all my battery-operated cameras at Georgia's. The local tech store was more expensive than going into one of the big box stores several towns over. But I didn't think we had time for that.

I knew one place that might have some extra. Sighing, I pulled out my cell and texted Hardy.

"I might be able to get some extra cameras, battery operated ones I don't have to connect to WIFI."

Mitch nodded. "Good idea. You have lots of great places to hide them."

"I have an idea for bait, too," I added. "There's a copy of the Audubon book on one of my shelves. It's not the original, not even close, but it might draw their eye and bring them in for a closer look."

"What do you need from me?" he asked.

"Maybe step out of the shop for a while, sometime later this afternoon. I'll let you know if my contact comes through with the cameras."

He tipped an imaginary hat to me. "I'll wait to hear."

Mitch held the tarp open for me to step through. "Be careful today. There's a lot of debris around. We'll make sure we clean up before we go, but it's a minefield right now."

I nodded my agreement and kept my eyes on the ground as I waded through it.

My cell pinged just as I made it back to the main shop.

Got them. Anything else?

I texted him about Liam meeting me at the station and asked if he could leave the cameras at the front desk so I could pick them up and get them installed before I had to come back.

He agreed, and I let out a breath of relief. I'd only have to see him once then.

Harper stared at me expectantly. "Anything?"

"We're doing a mini sting. I'm running to the police station to pick up a few extra cameras."

She winced. "Want me to do it?" Harper knew what happened with Hardy, but I never gave her all the details. Just the awful highlights.

"Nah. It's okay. Thanks, though. He's leaving them at the desk, so I'll grab them and hurry back here. Liam is meeting me later, so I need to hurry up and get them set up."

"Okay. The shop is pretty slow today. I can help you when you get back."

"Thanks, Harper." I hurried out of the shop.

True to his word, Hardy had left a small box full of cameras. Knowing him, the batteries were brand new and already installed. I thanked the receptionist and hurried back out the door.

A customer stepped out of Tattered Pages right when I got back. I smiled at her and hurried inside.

"You got them!" Harper hurried over and took the box from me. She set it on the register desk and pulled one out. They were small and black, perfect for the high corners of the shelving. I checked all the cameras and, sure enough, Hardy had put all new batteries in them.

My heart did a happy little lurch at his thoughtfulness, but I squashed it down.

Harper and I each took a few cameras and divided and conquered.

When we finished and had everything turned on, I searched through the box and found a slip of paper. Frowning, I picked it up and saw Hardy's slanted scrawl.

Dakota,

I don't know what's going on, but I suspect it relates to the current situation you're looking into. The batteries will last at least three weeks.

He listed an app I had to download and some troubleshooting instructions.

I squashed down that happy little lurch one more time and followed his instructions.

It took us a little longer than comfortable to get everything set up. I didn't mind tech, but I wasn't the best with it sometimes. But we finally had each camera loaded. I didn't know how this all worked, but I could flip to each camera and see it set up. Plus, it had a handy feature where it switched to WIFI if the batteries died. Once it was on WIFI, someone would be able to see it if they had some tech knowledge, but if the batteries lasted that long, it shouldn't be an issue.

Georgia's worked in a similar way, but I planned to go by there tomorrow and check the feed anyway.

In the meantime, I had a book to set up as a lure.

SIXTEEN

A tall, handsome man stepped out of a sleek blue Audi. He wore dark gray, slim cut slacks, a light blue button-down shirt with a gray and blue matching tie. His hair was cut short but not severe, but I couldn't see the color of his eyes due to the flattering sunglasses he wore.

A wide smile spread over my face as I rose from the bench outside the police department. "Liam!" I called.

His eyes found me, and he grinned, his perfect, straight white teeth just as bright as I remembered. He came over with a familiar, purposeful stride and brought me into a warm embrace. Liam smelled like the outdoors, fresh and clean. I discreetly took a sniff and resisted the urge to bury my nose into the crook of his neck.

He let me go and took a step back, still holding my shoulders. "Look at you. Just as gorgeous as I remember."

Heat colored my cheeks. "And you look like you've walked off the cover of a magazine. You look great, Liam.

It's wonderful to see you again. We need to catch up more often and not when I have to hire you."

Liam laughed. "I'm not hired yet. Tell me what it is you need."

I winced. "It's better if I show you."

His dark brows lifted. "Sounds mysterious." Liam held out his arm. "Lead on, then."

I curled my fingers around his elbow and let him lead me inside.

The woman at the receptionist desk stumbled over her words when she saw Liam walk in. I bit down my smile and asked her if Detective Cavanaugh was available. She nodded mutely and let us go through.

I snorted once I was out of hearing distance. "Still got that charm, don't you?"

Liam shook his head. "I didn't say a word."

"You never had to." And it was true.

Liam had a way about him that appealed to men and women alike. He was handsome, intelligent, and could carry a conversation even when no one else could. We were fast friends as soon as we met, and nothing had ever come between us.

He asked me out once, many years ago, but after a long talk, we both agreed it was best to stay friends. There was never any awkwardness between us afterward, and he never brought it up again.

We walked down the hall to Hardy's office.

Liam's neck was on a swivel, and he had a pep in his

step. "This is the most interesting thing to happen to me in years!"

I huffed a laugh. "It's here because I wasn't sure where else to put it."

"It would be...?" He wiggled his eyebrows at me.

"It's right down here." I stopped at the entrance to Hardy's office and knocked on the door.

Hardy opened it, smiled, then noticed Liam. His expression turned wary. "Dakota. Who's your friend?"

"Liam." He stuck his hand out. "Liam Manford. I'm an antiquarian."

One of Hardy's eyebrows went up. "And that would be?"

I rubbed my mouth to hide my smile.

"I authenticate books. Dakota said she had something to show me."

"Ah." Hardy's eyes cleared. "Come in then." He stepped away from the door and gestured for us to enter.

I stepped in first, Hardy's light cologne tickling my nose. My heart beat twice as fast as normal. Liam followed behind and stepped up beside me, his gaze going straight to the safe. His eyes flashed with interest.

"I hope whatever you want me to look at is inside that incredible safe."

Hardy shut the door behind us, turning the lock so we wouldn't be disturbed. "Do you need my assistance?" he asked me.

I shook my head. "No. Thank you for keeping it safe."

Hardy shrugged. "Anything for you."

Liam's brows flicked up, and he gave me a curious look.

Heat colored my cheeks. Clearing my throat, I tried to put my feelings about Hardy out of my mind and thought about the combination I'd earlier committed to memory. Once I had that in my head, I kneeled down and opened the safe, the click of the lock loud in the quiet room.

Liam had come over and sat beside me, his face rapt with interest.

I got to my knees and peered inside the safe, reaching for the envelope. Relief filled me when my fingers wrapped around the envelope. Not that anything would have happened to it inside the police station, but stranger things have happened.

Liam stood and held out a hand to help my rise. I took it, the warmth of his palm against mine. Hardy cleared his throat, but I ignored him. Liam's gesture was innocent, and I had nothing to feel guilty about. Also, I would never flirt with someone else in front of him. I wasn't that kind of person.

"Can I use this table?" I asked Hardy.

He stood and came over, his arm brushing against mine. "Of course." I helped him move everything off the table and onto the small round table next to his desk. Once that was finished, I pulled out an extra pair of cotton gloves I had shoved in my purse and pulled out one of the volumes, putting the envelope down before gently setting the book on top.

Liam sucked in a shocked breath, his eyes wide as they flicked from the book to me.

"My God, Dakota." His mouth opened and shut twice before he spoke again. "Do you know what this is?"

I tugged my gloves off and handed them to Liam. He wasted no time in donning them and opening the book with gentle reverence.

"Is this real?" I asked quietly.

Liam shook his head, his fingers trembling as he examined the pages. "I don't know." His voice sounded tight and strained. "If it is, you are in great danger, my dear."

Hardy stiffened. "Dakota?" His eyes went to the book. "I know this is valuable. But exactly how valuable?"

Liam flipped another page. "The last time this book went to auction, it went for almost ten million."

Hardy choked. "Ten—what?" His eyes found mine. "Million?" Hardy shoved a hand through his hair. "That's —" He blew out a long breath.

"Crazy, right?" Liam chuckled. "Dakota has made the find of the century."

"Maybe," I said.

Liam shook his head and stood, tugging the gloves off. "Not maybe. That's an original." He chuckled. "Who knows about this?"

"Hardy. My contractor knows I found something, but he has no idea what it is or how valuable it might be."

Liam nodded. "Who saw you move the safe out?"

Hardy blew out a breath. "A few people. Officers I trust."

"This piece belongs in a museum. Not in a police station."

Hardy snorted. "This is the safest place for it right now. It's too dangerous for Dakota to take it back."

"I agree." Liam crossed his arms over his chest. "How secure is the safe?"

Hardy shrugged. "It's over a thousand pounds. No one is getting it out of here without going to extreme effort."

I stared at Liam. "Are you saying..." My throat worked. "Is this—"

He nodded. "It's the real deal."

I swayed, the possibilities overwhelming me. "This—oh my goodness. It's real." I put my hand over my heart, the thumping beat of it like a rabbit's.

"Yeah." Liam chuckled. "This is the best find I've ever seen. Everyone is going to be so jealous."

Hardy took me by the elbow and led me to the comfy couch by his desk. "Sit for a moment."

I gratefully sank into the seat and leaned my head back. "Thanks."

His warm hand rested on my knee. "This is what the thief is looking for. You're sure of it?"

I nodded. "Ninety-five percent." A thought occurred to me. "I set up this same book inside my cabinet to see if whoever it is will bite."

"Who did you tell about the missing things?" Hardy asked.

"Harper called me. I talked to Mitch about it."

He nodded. "I'll drive you back to the shop once you're finished. We can check the cameras when we're there."

"Thanks, Hardy."

He nodded and squeezed my knee before he stood up and faced Liam. "I don't think I need to tell you how important it is to keep this quiet. If you endanger Dakota by running your mouth..." His voice trailed off.

Liam's brow furrowed. He looked at me then Hardy before his expression cleared. "Ah. I see," he said quietly. "You didn't tell me you were dating anyone, Dakota."

I closed my eyes for a moment before blinking away the tears threatening to form. "I'm not. Hardy and I broke up a few weeks ago."

Hardy stilled.

Liam nodded. "Makes sense. The room is a little tense." He winked at me and handed the gloves over.

I gave him a quelling look and snatched them from his hands. Carefully, I gathered the volume and slid it back into the envelope before I put everything back into the safe, ensuring I shut and locked it. I double checked it and stood, turning to face the two men.

"What should I do?" I asked Liam.

"I'll get you an authentication certificate." He shrugged. "More than likely, it will have to be authenticated again. The value is astronomical. But that can wait. For now, I'd call an auction house. Maybe Christie's?" Liam laughed. "I've never dealt with something of this magnitude. I can do some research and get back to you."

Hardy's look would have turned him to stone if it could have. "Soon," he growled.

Liam nodded. "Soon as I can. Is there a good hotel around here?"

Hardy gave him a couple of options. Our town had more bed and breakfasts than hotels, so Hardy told him the best one. Liam nodded, gave us a little salute, and waited for Hardy to unlock the door before he stepped out. "I'll call you later," he said, winking seconds before Hardy slammed the door in his face.

His bark of laughter came through the door.

"Unnecessary," I said.

Hardy lifted a shoulder in a shrug. "But cathartic." He perched on the edge of the table and studied me. "You're a millionaire, darling. What are you going to do?"

The thought of it made me ill. I shook my head. "Not a millionaire yet. I can't even think about it. This..." I waved my hand at the safe, "is terrifying. I can't even fathom that amount of money."

"Let's chat." He led me over to the couch and took his desk chair, rolling it closer to me. "Tell me everything. How you found the safe, how you realized what you have, and how you figured out what the thief is looking for."

I ran through the series of events, up until Mitch showed me the safe in the room and Hardy arrived. He took a few notes, stopping me every once in a while, murmuring things to himself, and gesturing for me to continue. "And the safe was on the Tattered Pages side?"

I nodded.

"And the clause in your contract is solid?"

"Solid as it can be. Honestly, I don't plan on giving my name out if I sell the thing. Keeping it is out of the question. I don't have the security I'd need to keep it safe." I sighed. "Or myself."

He nodded. "Your friend is right. Every weirdo in a hundred-mile radius will come sniffing around if they know you have that thing." Hardy rubbed his hand over his jaw, his eyes lost in thought. "I think we need to move the safe."

I blinked. "From the station?"

He shook his head. "Every single person we tell about this is one more person who might accidentally endanger your safety."

"Liam wouldn't—" I began.

Hardy held his hand up. "I don't know your friend, Dakota. But I have to be honest. I don't care about him. I care about you. If he lets even a hint slip of what you have, you'll be in grave danger."

He wasn't wrong. Liam was stoked when he walked out of here. If he said something in his excitement, it might mean the end of me.

"I know things are strained between us right now, but I think you need protection. I'd like to stay with you this evening."

My heart lurched. "Hardy, I don't think—"

"I sent Maria away." He sighed. "My daughter stayed with me. She's with her grandmother right now until I get a few things straightened out."

I didn't want to ask, but his eyes lit up when he said the word *daughter*. "How is it? Being a dad?"

Our eyes met and held.

He took a deep breath. "Everything I never knew I wanted."

A breath escaped me. Tears pricked the back of my eyes. "Oh. Hardy, that's wonderful."

He ducked his head and looked away for a second. "It's not the way I wanted it to happen, but she's an amazing kid."

"She's your daughter. Of course she is." We smiled at each other.

And for the first time in weeks, I relaxed.

SEVENTEEN

Hardy followed me back to the store. By that time, the sun had slipped below the horizon, and darkness had fallen over Silverwood. Mitch and his contractors were long gone, and Harper had left hours ago. He motioned for me to stay in the car while he got out and did a quick perimeter check.

When Hardy came back, he opened the vehicle door and helped me out. Harper had left a lamp light on, the golden glow highlighting the store with warmth.

The clever girl had moved the lamp to showcase the locked cabinet. The Birds of America volume was still there, the case still locked tight.

Hardy nudged me behind him, his hand resting on the butt of his gun. He carefully navigated his way through the shop, me following close behind him. Once he'd inspected every nook and cranny in the store, his posture relaxed.

"It's safe." He turned to face me. "Where are the cameras?"

I walked him through the store and let him collect the cameras. He double-checked everything to ensure they were all working, then pulled the memory cards out.

"Got somewhere we can look at this?"

I led him behind the desk and showed him the store laptop. Hardy waited for me to log in and slide it over. With a few taps, he was in, flipping through footage.

"Want some coffee?" I asked.

"Have any decaf?"

"I do. I'll make a fresh pot."

"Thanks."

A few minutes later, the scent of fresh coffee permeated the store. I set a fresh mug in front of Hardy who grunted his thanks and made myself comfortable on the couch.

"Nothing on the first one," he said, slipping a new card in.

"I doubt they'd come back this soon."

"Never discount a criminal's eagerness to meet their goals."

I snorted and sipped my coffee, waiting for him to get through the next one.

By the third, I was nodding off. Outside, the town was in full darkness, a few streetlights illuminating the town square.

"One more," Hardy said, jerking me out of my sleepy reverie.

"Thank goodness," I muttered.

His teeth flashed white. "I'll be back first thing in the morning with an officer."

"It's not necessary."

He looked over at me. "You're worth millions, Dakota."

"Maybe. But no one knows it yet."

Hardy grunted. "Not yet. There are too many people involved in this for my comfort. How soon will Liam get you the certificate?"

I shrugged. "Probably tomorrow."

"What's your next step?"

"I've never done this before, but I assume I'll need to take it to someone who's discreet and handles sales like this." I sat up abruptly. Why hadn't I thought of this earlier?

"Dakota?"

"Daniel. I'll take it to Daniel. He'll be able to help."

Hardy's face darkened. They didn't like each other much. Hardy rightly suspected Daniel was interested in me. Daniel didn't like how Hardy treated me.

"He's the best choice," I said quietly. "He's already filthy rich."

Hardy snorted. "Even rich people commit crimes to get more money."

"He wouldn't." Daniel was sometimes uncomfortable with the level of his wealth. He'd want for nothing ever again. "I trust him."

"I don't like it."

"You mean you don't like him," I teased.

His lips tightened. "And if I say you're right?"

"You don't have to." I chuckled. "It's written all over your face."

"He wants more than friendship," Hardy growled.

"And he hasn't made a secret of it," I argued. "But he's never once pushed my boundaries. Daniel is aware all I'm capable of right now is friendship."

I realized what I said when Hardy's attention jerked from the camera to me. "Right now?"

We needed to have this conversation. I didn't want to have it, but it was necessary.

"We are no longer dating. Eventually, I might want to date again. Not now. Not even in the immediate future. But someday."

Hardy took a deep breath and blew it out. "I know," was all he said.

"So many things have changed. You've changed. You have this entirely new life, and I'm not involved in it."

"You could be," he said softly.

"I need time. You've had a bomb drop into your life. A lovely one, but a shock, nonetheless. You're a father now. But I'm not sure I'm prepared to be more than I am. To anyone." I flopped back onto the couch. "I'm not even sure if I want to have children. I'm older, there are things I want to do, places I want to see, and now..." I smiled up at the ceiling. "If this thing I have is real, those are all things I can do." Shaking my head, I looked over at him. "All I ever wanted was for you to be happy. However, you need to make that happen will make me happy. But I need time to adjust to this new normal."

"And you need time to figure out if you still want me in the picture."

My face softened. "Oh, Hardy. The thought of you not in the picture breaks my heart. But I think you need time, too. You need to figure out how to be a dad. I would be a distraction to that. We both know it. The wisest thing we could do is keep a friendly distance." I waved my hand. "The current issue notwithstanding. Maybe try to get to know each other again once we both realize who we are without each other."

He nodded, grief flashing in his eyes. "I know you're right, but I don't have to like it."

I laughed. "Neither do I. But we're both too old to jump headfirst into something. There's someone else to think about now, isn't there?"

Hardy's eyes crinkled at the edges when he smiled. His mouth opened but snapped shut. His brow furrowed. "Found something," he barked, his posture straightening. "Come over here."

I scrambled off the couch and hurried over to stand next to him.

"Here," he said, pointing to a corner of the video. There was shadowy movement close to the new door connecting the shops. "The image isn't crisp enough to see who it is."

"Plus they're wearing a hoodie," I observed, pointing to the curved edges of the person's head. Their face was obscured in the shadows. He or she carefully kept away from the lamp light. I'd placed the camera facing the door, but it was like the person knew it was there or suspected I had new ones.

Hardy peered closer. "Male," he observed. "At least six feet. Thin." He frowned. "You have the cameras set up outside?"

"The regular ones, yes."

"Show me," Hardy urged.

I opened the app on my cell, accessed the cameras, and handed it over. Hardy flipped through, occasionally pausing and fast-forwarding. "No vehicle access. He walked up from town. Toward the north."

"Does it mean anything?"

"Could be a local," he observed. "Or it could be someone staying in one of the bed and breakfasts that way." He handed my phone back. "I'll call and get a roster of everyone from the last few weeks. It might narrow things down some."

"Good idea. What can I do?"

"I'm going to head back to the office and get you a few more cameras. Do you mind if I access the shop with my keys?"

I shook my head. "Keep them for now."

"Is the access door to the expansion locked?"

"No." I frowned. "I should do that, right?"

Hardy laughed. "You should. Wait until the construction crew is done and do it after they leave for good."

"All right. Anything else?"

"Yes. Text me when you head to the shop until we get this taken care of. Better yet, share your location with me."

My eyes narrowed.

Hardy's eyes twinkled with amusement. "Not for any nefarious purposes, Dakota. We never shared it when we were dating, but this is different. You have millions someone is trying to get. I'd like to know where you are until we catch this guy."

"Are you willing to share yours?"

His smile widened. "Tit for tat?"

"Something like that. I have no issues with you knowing where I am at any time." He pulled out his cell, punched a few buttons, and my cell pinged, telling me Hardy had shared his location.

Just that easy. My heart melted a little. "Show me?"

Hardy took mine and did the same thing. "I put it on sharing indefinitely for both of us. When this is over, I'll show you how to turn it off if you can't figure it out."

I tucked my phone back into my pocket. "Thanks."

He nodded and closed the laptop. "I'll walk you out if you're ready."

"Let me put the laptop away, and I'll follow you out."

EIGHTEEN

I called Daniel around ten the next morning. He was on a deadline, so I didn't dare call before then. Even so, when he answered, he sounded groggy.

"I hope I didn't wake you up."

His grunt made me laugh. "Haven't had enough coffee."

"I won't keep you. There's something I need to discuss with you, but I don't want to do it over the phone."

There was a long pause. When he spoke again, the grogginess had left his voice. "Are you in trouble?"

Was I? "Yes and no."

Daniel huffed a laugh. "Figures. Okay. If I wasn't up before, I am now. When can you make it over?"

"How about forty-five minutes with hot coffee and donuts?"

"God bless you, woman. I'll hold you to it."

"See you soon."

"Can't wait."

I hung up the phone, warmth blooming in my stomach. Daniel sounded like he meant it. Sighing, I tucked my phone in my purse, gave Poppy a scratch behind the ears, and headed to get Daniel and myself some fuel for the day.

I juggled a cupholder of coffee and two large boxes of a mix of donuts. I loved the blueberry, Daniel loved the cinnamon twists. I'd never tried the strawberry or the Bavarian cream, so I added those and a few other interesting ones to the boxes.

Daniel answered on the first ring, flinging the door open and taking the boxes from me without a word. I followed him inside, kicking the door shut. He dug through the first box, smiled when he saw the cinnamon twists, plucked one out and took a huge bite.

He still hadn't said a word.

I pushed a coffee over, keeping an arm's length away from him. He grunted and pulled it toward him, popping the lid off, and taking a long sip.

I waited, nibbling on my blueberry donut.

Eventually, he deigned to speak. "Almost there." He took the other cinnamon twist and held up his index finger.

Shaking my head, I got up, coffee in hand, and walked outside, through the open patio doors. He'd find me when he was ready. Daniel had a ton of land, beautifully landscaped and green. The weather was turning cooler every single day, but there was no chance of snow yet. I'd never been here during colder weather, but I bet the place looked like a winter wonderland.

I headed for the porch swing set up several feet away from the house. My coffee still steamed from the lid, the fragrance of hazelnuts wafting through the air. The early morning air was brisk against my skin, so I didn't push off and swing, merely sat and waited.

Amusement filled me at how grumpy Daniel was before coffee. He must have been up extremely late last night.

I hoped he was working on a new series. Daniel was the complete package. Tall, handsome, intelligent, and he wrote the best books I'd ever read.

Being so irritable in the morning knocked him down a few pegs and made him more human in my eyes.

I lifted my legs and let the gentle wind move the swing in a slight sway, enough to send a chill down my spine but not enough to spill my coffee.

It took Daniel another ten minutes before he stepped into the doorframe and waved at me to come back in.

Grinning, I hopped off the swing and headed back inside.

He'd started on the second coffee I brought him. That one was a honey lavender latte. His brows lifted in surprise. "Mmm. That's odd but good." He waved his coffee at me. "Sorry. It's early, and I had a late night. Come sit beside me and tell me what's wrong."

Daniel plopped onto the couch, careful not to spill his coffee, and patted the place beside him. Rolling my eyes, I settled into the chair opposite.

His lips curved into a smile. "What is it this time? Mayhem? Chaos? Thefts, murders, despair?"

"I think I'm a millionaire," I blurted.

Daniel blinked. He stared at me for a long moment. "I think you need to start at the beginning."

When I finished, Daniel scratched his chin and blew out a long breath. "Holy smokes." He shook his head and chuckled. "Only you, Dakota."

"What do I do?" My voice came out whiny. I snapped my jaw shut and started again. "I am freaking out inside. By rights, what's in the safe is mine, but what do I do? How do I sell the thing and get them to keep it a secret? I don't have the security to keep it safe at the shop and certainly not at my house."

During the last case I worked, someone had broken into my house rendering it unsafe until we solved it. I was forced to move into Hardy's guesthouse, making it even more awkward when everything happened. The thought of trying to secure those volumes inside my house was laughable.

"You have options," Daniel said. He never freaked out about anything. Every time I saw him, he was calm, cool, and collected.

"It's at the police station. That's my only option."

"You can have the safe moved here." Daniel rose and motioned for me to follow. We walked past his incredible library, though my steps slowed as I peered inside and sighed at the smell of aged paper and wisdom. Daniel tugged my arm. "We'll visit on the way back," he said dryly. "The books have missed you too."

I grinned at his back and let him pull me down the hall.

We took so many turns I lost all hope of finding my way back. Eventually, we stopped at a tall metal door. I gave Daniel a curious look. He gave me a mysterious smile and pulled it open, the weight of the door groaning with the movement.

He flipped on the light and walked inside.

I peered in, my eyes widening at the sight. Four massive safes sat at the back of the wall, two antique, and two modern. Multiple shelves were built into the walls, full of miscellaneous knick-knacks, folders, and...gold bars?

"Daniel. Is that gold?" I laughed out loud. "Who are you? A pirate?"

He shrugged. "Dad was paranoid."

"I'll say."

He tapped one of the shelves. "Come closer to me and away from the door."

I gave him a wary glance but did as he asked. He turned me away from him, one arm wrapped around my waist. "Watch," he whispered in my ear. Gooseflesh rose on my arms.

I felt him move behind me. Seconds later, a whirring noise came from all directions. A moment after that, metal barriers slammed down all around us.

I squeaked with fright, bumping into Daniel's chest. The lights went out, plunging us into immediate darkness.

"Daniel?"

"Don't worry. Wait a moment." His arm was heavy over my waist, breath warm against my neck.

A clicking noise sounded, the room becoming awash in a golden glow. I gasped in surprise.

Daniel let go and stepped away, walking to the other side of the room to turn on a second lamp. "This place acts as a panic room. It's the safest spot in my house. Dad has more than one similar area here, but this one is my favorite."

"Rich people," I said fondly, making Daniel laugh.

"It took me years to figure this place out, but I occasionally still find new things inside that surprise me."

"How does it lock?"

Daniel reached over and touched something. The metal barriers moved back into the ceiling and disappeared. "I can activate those while outside the room. If you choose to move the safe here, I'll ensure they're active all the time until we find the right person to sell the books for you."

He pulled the door open, and we stepped outside. "The lock is electronic, controlled by an app only I have access to."

I ran my fingers over the metal. "Electronic?"

"I'll show you once I close it."

Daniel grunted as he pushed it closed. Once I was several feet away, he pulled his cell out, pressed a few things, and several, loud clanking noises sounded from inside the room. Then it hissed, clanked one more time, and silence fell.

"Try to open it," he said.

I gave him a dubious look. "It probably wouldn't budge even if I tried."

"Try anyway," he said.

Shrugging, I walked up to it, pulled the round handle, and tugged as hard as I could.

Nothing. I braced my foot against the wall and tried again.

No dice.

"I'm not sure if this is a testament to the strength of the lock," I said with a grunt. "My arms have the strength of wet spaghetti noodles."

Daniel grinned. "They'll hold up to a lot more than wet noodles."

"It's safer than the police station?"

Daniel gave me an amused look before he shrugged. "The room is. Obviously, I'm not a highly trained law enforcement officer, but money does buy safety. This space is impenetrable and inaccessible from the outside even if someone rammed a car into the house."

I blinked and looked up at him. "Is someone ramming a car into your house a common occurrence?"

He snorted. "No. But if they tried, they still wouldn't make it to the safe room."

It was an appealing proposition. I wouldn't have to see Hardy all the time, and I'd feel good that the volumes were in such a secure space. "How long do you think you'd have to store them?"

"Not long." He took my elbow and led me back to the kitchen. "Something like that would go fast. Do you have it authenticated?"

I nodded. "I have a friend who is also an authenticator. He came by and took a look. I should have the certificate soon."

"Good. That will speed things up, though I assume the auction house will have one of their authenticators take a look, especially since you're friends with the one you used."

He held the coffee pot up with a questioning look.

"No thanks." I'd already finished my latte, but I wasn't in the mood for more.

"I can make a couple of calls while you're still here and see how soon I can get someone to come and look at the volumes. Is Hardy available for us to come by?"

"I'll ask." I sent him a message and waited.

Hardy texted back quickly. "He has a short appointment in half an hour but said it should take less than an hour total. Meeting around lunch time should work."

Daniel nodded and went to work.

An hour later, I was sprawled on his couch flipping through one of his new works in progress. Daniel wrote like he was in the middle of a fever dream. The pages he printed out were pristine initially, but he'd written notes all over the place—in the margins, in the middle of the text, top, bottom...it didn't seem to matter. I couldn't read half of them, and I had no idea how he planned to keep all of it straight.

Obviously, he could. Daniel was pretty famous, so his system worked for him.

To me, it looked like a trainwreck.

He disconnected another call. "I found an available authenticator. Sylvia will meet us at the police station at one. On my word, she's bringing paperwork so she can take the Aububon book back with her."

I winced. "How will she protect it?"

Daniel gave me a long look. "Is there something else you want to tell me?"

"I think someone is looking for it. They think it's somewhere in the area." I told Daniel about the ongoing thefts and my suspicions about what they were looking for.

One of Daniel's eyebrows went up. "And they're on the right track." He rubbed his chin. "Think Hardy could give her an escort?"

"That seems like a big ask."

Daniel chuckled. "Not if you're the one doing the asking."

I gave him a look, but he shrugged. "It's a big deal. Sylvia will be escorting millions of dollars in merchandise. If someone is actively looking for it, there's a chance they might have figured out where it is and are just looking for the right moment to take it."

"Better safe than sorry," we said at the same time.

"Let's see if she thinks they're the real deal. I'll put the idea in Hardy's mind and see if he agrees. They're shorthanded on officers right now, so let's hope it's a slow day."

Daniel snagged another donut. "It's never a slow day when you're involved, Dakota."

I glared, snatching the donut out of his hand and taking a huge bite.

He snatched it back and shoved the rest of it in his mouth, spraying crumbs at my squawk of protest. In response, I pulled the box closer and stuck my tongue out at him.

Daniel chewed, his chest shaking with laughter. When he finished chewing, he took a sip of coffee. "We have some time. Want to explore the rest of the grounds?"

"As long as we get to spend some time in the library before we have to go."

"Promise."

I wrapped my fingers around the crook in his arm and let him lead me out.

Daniel drove like an elderly person. I passed by, driving the speed limit and did a scrunch face at him. He threw his head back laughing as I sailed past. Shaking my head, I stopped paying attention to his road antics and headed straight for the police station.

Hardy texted me right before we left to let me know he was on his way back and would meet us at the front to escort us in.

When I pulled into the lot, he was already outside, scanning the lot for our vehicles.

He jogged over once he saw mine and pulled the door open for me. "Daniel drives like an old lady, so he's at least five minutes out."

Hardy reached in and grabbed my sweater. "It's chilly. Here."

He helped me put it on, gently brushing my hair out of the way. I closed my eyes and held in my sigh. If only things were different. Maybe one day the universe would align for us.

"Do you want to wait outside?"

"We can. It's nice today." The sun had come out a while ago, warming the temperatures some, but it was still frigid outside. The walk around Daniel's property had chilled me from head to toe, but I'd cranked the heat all the way up on the drive over, focusing most of the warmth on thawing my toes out.

I really needed to get some lined boots. Every year, I thought about it, and every year I failed to get a pair. Silverwood Hollow didn't have a big mall or even a regular department store. We had to drive forty-five minutes to reach a big box store, so most of the time I ordered things online, sometimes with mixed results.

"Daniel has another authenticator coming. If it's real, we'll sign the paperwork today and she will take it with her." I peered up at him hopefully. "Would you mind providing an escort?"

"No problem." Hardy leaned against the wall, his jacket collar popped up to protect his neck from the cold.

"Thanks. I'd love to buy you dinner as a thank you."

His eyes flashed. "I'll take you up on that provided you come with it."

My cheeks flushed. "Erm. I'll go to dinner. Not be dinner."

His grin told me I shouldn't be so sure of that. I huffed a laugh. Daniel pulled in just as Hardy was about to say something else. Relieved, I turned away and headed down the steps. A sleek silver car followed behind him.

He parked, the other vehicle pulling in right next to him.

A tall woman with sleek dark hair stepped out, her high heels clicking on the pavement. She had the look of the big city about her. Her hair spilled over her shoulders, and she wore minimal makeup, but a dark berry-colored lip and mascara. To be fair, she was stunning and didn't even need the minimal amount she wore. Daniel got out next, smiling at the woman I assumed was Sylvia.

"This is Dakota," he said, tilting his head in my direction. "Next to her is Hardy Cavanaugh. If everything works out, he will be the one escorting you back to wherever you go when you're taking merchandise back."

Sylvia nodded to me, her dark eyes taking my measure, before turning to Hardy. Her eyes lingered longer on him, approval flashing in their dark depths. A sting of jealousy uncurled in my stomach, but I squashed it down. He and I weren't together. If he was interested, then so be it.

"The item is inside?" she asked in a lightly accented voice.

"It is." I glanced up at Hardy who, surprisingly, wasn't paying attention to Sylvia. Instead, his attention was directed at me.

"It's in my office." Her jerked his head toward the building. "Follow me."

The woman's eyes widened when she saw the safe, so I

can only imagine how she might react when she saw the volumes.

"Do you want the safe?" she asked.

I hadn't even thought about it. On one hand, it was a bear to move, but I could put a lot of valuable things inside of it and not worry about them going anywhere.

"I haven't decided yet. If I decide to get rid of it, would you like me to call you?"

"I would."

"I'll do that. But for right now, I'm more interested in selling what's inside." My email had gone off a little earlier with the certificate attached, so I had that, but Sylvia hadn't said anything yet. Nor had she arrived with her authenticator.

"I thought you had someone to authenticate this coming?" I asked as I bent down to open the safe. Everyone stood a far enough distance away that I didn't worry about anyone seeing the combination.

"Yes. He will be here in a few minutes. Something came up at his hotel. He is on the way as we speak."

I looked over my shoulder. "Should I wait until he comes?"

Sylvia frowned. "That's unnecessary. I am well-trained in spotting fakes. Bryan is only the final step. I will have a good idea even without him here."

"All right then." The last number clicked into place, and I pushed down on the handle. The envelopes lay stacked just how I'd left them. I took them out and put them on the table. Once I had the gloves on, I took out each volume, one by one, and lay them beside each other on the table.

Sylvia's breath came out in a soft gasp. She turned away and pulled her cellphone out, her fingers tapping on the screen.

I pulled the gloves off and handed them to her when she turned back around. She'd wiped all expression off her face, accepted the gloves, and tugged them on. Sylvia tied her hair up with a clear tie I hadn't noticed on her wrist. She pulled out a pair of glasses and perched them on her nose, then bent to study each volume.

"This might take a bit. Feel free to do something else."

Hardy snorted. "We'll wait right here."

Annoyance flashed over her face, but she stayed silent.

I agreed with Hardy. There was no way I was leaving these unattended.

He pulled a chair over for me and grabbed one for himself. Daniel rolled his eyes and plopped down on the couch by the desk.

Silence ticked between us. The occasional sound of a page flip was the only noise besides the click of the air conditioner. About fifteen minutes later, a sharp knock came from outside. Hardy rose and opened the door, murmuring something to the person standing there.

He stepped aside and a man entered—tall, thin, and... familiar. His watery blue eyes raked over me in dismissal as he headed straight for Sylvia. The man wore a fedora, disguising most of his hair.

I pulled out my cell and sent Hardy a text.

I've seen him before.

His head shot up, our eyes meeting. *Where?*

I can't remember.

He nodded. "What was your name again?" Hardy asked.

The man turned. "Me?"

"Yes." Hardy waited.

"Bryan."

"Bryan...?"

Irritation flashed in his eyes. "Boyd."

"And are you with an organization?"

Bryan nodded. "McIntosh Rare Books in Springfield."

Hardy tilted his head. "Springfield is a hike from here. I assume you were already close?"

The man stiffened. "Visiting family two towns over. I do occasional work for Sylvia."

"Nice to meet you," Hardy said. He rattled off his name, helpfully mentioning his role in the police department.

Bryan's lips thinned. "Good to know." He pulled a pair of thin cotton gloves from his briefcase and slid them on. "Miss Adair, we will have an answer soon."

I settled back into my chair and prepared to wait all over again.

Hardy watched Bryan with interest, his keen eyes missing nothing.

It took them another half hour before Sylvia straightened, a wide smile on her stunning face. "Well, it appears this is the real deal."

I blinked. It was one thing to suspect it, but another thing entirely to know it was real. This could change my entire life.

My mouth opened and snapped shut. I inhaled and exhaled, but still couldn't form the words.

"What happens next?" Hardy asked.

I sent him a wordless thank you gesture.

Sylvia pulled the gloves off and accessed a sheath of papers from her purse. "We fill all this out and sign it. I'll take some photographs, then I'll need to transport the volumes to the auction house. I'll call them in a few minutes, once we get everything signed." She sent me a hopeful smile. "You ready to get the ball rolling?"

I nodded. How in the world had I gotten so lucky?

"Will these be insured in case something happens?"

Sylvia nodded. "We carry a policy. The documents are also in there." She opened the folder and pulled out the first bundle. "Now, let's get this finished. I'm sure the auction house will be delighted once we bring everything in. There's an auction this weekend. I'm sure they'll find a place for these even if they have to bump something else."

Bryan picked his briefcase up. "If that's all?"

Sylvia held up a finger. "I have the certificate here. Wait just a moment."

The next half hour was filled with paperwork, stamps, and enough signatures to make my head spin. When it was all over, Sylvia smiled and put her hand out for me to shake. "It was wonderful doing business with you. I'll be in touch very soon." She leaned forward. "If you ever find anything else you're interested in selling, please feel free to reach out."

Sylvia tucked a card into my hand, smiled, and stacked all the volumes into a file box.

Hardy pulled his jacket on, over his service weapon. "I'll escort her home. Once I'm on the road, I'll let you know."

Daniel had stayed quiet the entire time. He unfolded his length from the couch and stood. "I'll follow behind the caravan if you don't mind."

"Oh!" I said in surprise. "That's unnecessary."

Daniel shrugged. "It's an added layer of protection. Plus, I want to see this famous warehouse Sylvia is always talking about. Volumes like that can't be left unprotected, so I wonder what kind of security they have set up."

Sylvia's lips thinned. "I assure you, I will take the utmost care with her property."

Daniel shrugged. "I'm sure you will, but one more set of eyes won't hurt, will it?"

Bryan headed across the room. "If you require further services," he said to Sylvia, "please reach out."

He slipped out the door and was gone before anyone could respond.

"Strange man," I remarked.

Sylvia laughed. "He's good at what he does, though. That's all anyone can ask."

"I suppose so." It was still bothering me that I couldn't place him. I know I'd seen him before.

Daniel picked up the box. "Want to take this with you, Hardy?" he asked.

Hardy glanced at the box. "I think that's a good idea." He took the outstretched box and tucked it under his arm.

Sylvia frowned. "I can travel with it."

Hardy slowly shook his head. "Someone will think twice before they attack a police car."

"Attack?" Sylvia blanched. "Why would they do that?"

"Money makes people do crazy things," Hardy said.

Seeing reason, Sylvia waved her hand. "Fine. But drive carefully."

Hardy snorted. "I'm the very picture of careful," he drawled.

Daniel gave me a look. "I'll text you when we're on the way back. My fee is an extra chess night this month."

"Deal," I said, just as Hardy's jaw tightened in annoyance.

I needed to get away from these two for my own peace of mind. "Thank you both for this. Sylvia, thanks for coming out this way and taking the time to look at these volumes."

In a surprise flash of good humor, Sylvia laughed. "Are you kidding? This was the find of the century. I would have ridden a tricycle out here."

We grinned at each other. Hardy and Daniel headed out, and I followed behind, breathing a sigh of relief now that these things were finally off my hands. "Can I keep the safe in here for a few more days while I try to figure out how to get it back to the shop?'

Hardy locked the door behind us. "No worries. Keep it here for as long as you need."

"Thanks."

He winked and turned to follow Daniel and Sylvia out the door.

On my way to the car, I noticed Bryan waiting in his vehicle a few rows from mine. He watched Sylvia and the others drive away before starting his vehicle and following behind. Frowning, I watched for a moment. He never said anything about going back with them.

Before I tried to rationalize my paranoia, I sent a text to Hardy letting him know that I thought Bryan had waited for them. He sent me a quick note back before I put it out of my head and drove home.

TWENTY

I was polishing off my last bite of baked chicken when my phone dinged, alerting me to new movement on Georgia's cameras. Pulling the cell over, I clicked the app to bring it up and nearly dropped my fork.

Someone was prowling through her store. I couldn't zoom in or anything, not with the live feed, so I watched it for a minute or two before I jumped up from my seat and shoved my feet into a pair of fuzzy slippers and headed out the door to my car.

In my head, I knew that by the time I arrived, whoever it was would be long gone, but I took off anyway at a high clip of speed. I voice called Hardy, but it went straight to voice mail. He was still on the way back from the escort trip, but I wanted someone to know where I was going.

I remembered he had access to my location, so I sent him a voice message letting him know about the camera.

Copper Canyon was calm and quiet when I pulled onto the main street. I slowed my speed and pulled into a parking spot two blocks away from Georgia's shop. I'd texted her while I was on my way, but she hadn't responded yet.

Shoving down worry for her, I hurried over to the shop, keeping my eyes peeled for anyone on the streets. The camera footage had continued going, and it appeared like the person was still inside. Whether there was a delay, I couldn't say, but I'd figure it out soon enough when I got there.

I tiptoed closer to the door, and when I stood at the edge, I peered into the window.

There was so much stuff in the window display, I couldn't see in. I thought she had a bell over the door, so going in would immediately alert someone to my presence. Grimacing, I moved away from the window and hurried to the back door.

When I saw it was propped open, dread pooled in my stomach. I stopped in my tracks, my breath puffing out in steam as I thought about my next steps. Going in might be foolish, but Georgia had yet to respond to my messages. If she were in there, she might be hurt. If I could help her, I should. But if she wasn't here, then I might be walking straight into something I was unprepared for.

Times like these, I wished Hardy were here. He'd be angry I put myself into this situation, but every time I was with him, I felt safe.

Squaring my shoulders, I exhaled quietly and tiptoed into the back of the store. While the front of the store was neat and tidy, the back area was a large, cluttered room filled with stacks of boxes and miscellaneous clutter. The lights were off back here, and every step was an exercise in agility. Long shadows crept along the walls, freaking me out at every single turn. I watched where I stepped while trying to keep my eyes ahead for the intruder. I'd just turned a corner when I heard the unmistakable rumble of a male voice.

"Where are they?" the man growled.

"Where is what?" Georgia said, exasperation coloring her tone.

"The books!"

Despite the danger we were both in, I bit down a smile when Georgia's annoyed squawk floated back to me. "We're in a bookstore!" she exclaimed with deep exasperation. "Take your pick!"

"The bird books!" the voice barked. "Where are they?"

Georgia sounded flabbergasted. "You stole all of them already! Honest to goodness, if you're going to rob me, I have fifty bucks in the register! Take it and leave. If you're going to do worse, I'm not going down without a fight."

"All I want are the books. Give them to me and I'll leave." The voice sounded muffled and hoarse, almost like he was trying to disguise it.

"And like I said before, you are in a bookstore, sir!"

I stepped back into the shadows and sent Hardy

another text telling him what was happening. He hadn't responded yet, but hopefully he would get the messages and send a unit out.

Until then, I had to help Georgia.

"The Audubon books. Where are they?"

"Nonfiction section," Georgia said, her voice wobbling. "They're all alphabetized!"

The man made a growl of frustration. "The originals!"

"I don't have any originals! My bookstore doesn't carry many rare books. Every once in a while, I'll find something I'll pick up to sell, but it doesn't happen often."

Something shattered. Georgia let out a wail of fear. I scanned the room I was in, looking for anything. My eyes landed on something that looked like a broom, but when I got closer, I realized it was one of those long-handled window cleaner things.

There was one door between me and Georgia. Wrapping my fingers around the handle, I slowly pulled it up, holding it like a baseball bat.

I inhaled a deep breath and stepped out from the back room, careful to hold the door so it wouldn't click shut. With careful hands, I gently rested the door against the jam and came up behind the man. Georgia's eyes widened a hair when she saw me, but she was a quick thinker and looked away, then opened her mouth and let out a loud wail.

"I can't help you! Let me go!" she cried.

I hefted the tool up and swung.

The would-be thief grunted and sank like a stone,

hitting the carpeted floor with a soft thunk. I stared at him for a long moment, my breath heaving in my chest, before dropping the tool and hurrying over to untie Georgia.

The front door flung open, revealing Hardy and another uniformed officer. I stooped over, my fingers working at the knots in the rope securing Georgia.

Hardy swore under his breath and hurried over to me, pulling me against his chest. My face smooshed against him, his fresh scent comforting.

"I'm going to yell at you for endangering yourself later, but I am so glad you're okay."

"Georgia needs medical attention," I muttered against his chest.

He pulled away, frowning down at me before he bent and cut Georgia's bindings away.

The other officer drew his gun and stood over the downed burglar, who was still out cold. He glanced up at me in surprise. "You walloped him a good one, didn't you?"

I shrugged. "He deserved it."

The man laughed as he extricated his handcuffs. "I suppose he did." Unceremoniously, the officer turned the man onto his stomach and cuffed his wrists. Once he was secure, he checked the man's pockets before calling for an ambulance.

Georgia grimaced and rubbed her wrists. "Thank you so much. How in the world did you know I needed help?"

I shook my head. "I didn't. The camera app pinged. I saw someone in here who wasn't supposed to be, so I got in the car and headed over. I called Hardy on the way here."

She stood, shaking off the bindings, and reached for me, dragging me into a one-armed hug. "You and I should go to lunch soon. My treat." Georgia sighed and rubbed her face. "As much as I'm relieved you're here, I have a feeling this isn't over."

I had to agree. Hardy grunted. "He'll need to get cleared medically, but once he is, we'll get to the bottom of it. It's possible he's the culprit behind all of it, but I tend to agree with you. I think there's more than one person."

"Me too," I said.

Red and blue lights flickered against the walls as the ambulance pulled up. I took Georgia's arm and led her over to the seating area. Once she was situated, I busied myself making tea. When the water boiled, I poured out four cups, added a bag of peppermint to hers, and set it on the table in front of her. I chose Earl Grey and the same for Hardy, but I gave the other officer a cup of Oolong. Why, I didn't know. He just looked like an Oolong guy.

They both accepted the steaming mugs gratefully just as the doors opened and EMTs flooded in. The men headed straight for the man on the ground, but Hardy directed them to Georgia.

"Check her first, please."

One frowned, but they both turned to do as he asked.

Two other officers stepped inside the shop, gazes scanning the room for danger before landing on Hardy.

They walked over and dove into a quiet conversation I couldn't make out.

I sipped my tea as the EMTs worked on Georgia, but it

didn't take long. "Just some scrapes and bruises, ma'am. Nothing serious. I'd recommend taking some over-the-counter pain meds before you go to bed. You'll be a little sore tomorrow, but I don't see anything serious here."

Georgia's smile looked wan. "Thank you both."

"No problem, ma'am," said the younger one.. Soon enough, they made the decision to load the guy up on the stretcher and wheel him out. Once that happened, Hardy returned his attention to us. "We won't be too much longer. Mack will need to ask you a few questions, but overall, this looks pretty cut and dry."

"Mack?" I questioned.

Hardy jerked his thumb over his shoulder. "The officer who came in with me."

Mack waved. I chuckled. "All right. He was in here for a while before I arrived. Georgia is the one who knows the most."

"You just came in and went all ninja on him?" Hardy asked, amusement curving his lips up.

"Not even ninja," I admitted. "Whacking him on the back of the head was way easier than I expected it to be."

Hardy laughed at that. "You hit him perfectly to drop him like that. Good job, Dakota."

A warm flush of pleasure sent tingles to my toes. It shouldn't be the kind of thing that made me feel proud of myself, but knowing I'd protected myself and Georgia and that Hardy recognized it, too, gave me a sense of purpose I hadn't felt in a while.

How I felt made zero sense, but it was late, and it

didn't have to. Even I was surprised he dropped so quickly, but that window cleaner pole was pretty substantial, if I said so myself.

Mack came over and sat by Georgia. He held a small notepad and wrote occasional notes down as she spoke. We waited, sipping our tea, until Mack turned his attention to me. I ran down everything that happened, including how I discovered she was in danger. When I told him I didn't realize the danger she was in until I went into the store, his brows lifted. "You deliberately grabbed the window cleaner to strike him?"

"Well, yes. He had Georgia, and it was the only thing I could find to distract him."

Mack laughed. "You didn't quite distract him."

"Well, yes," I agreed with a wry laugh. "Knocking him out was the best-case scenario, as far as I can tell."

Georgia nodded eagerly. "I agree. Dakota is welcome to come into my store and knock any other prowlers out any time she wants to."

Hardy snorted. "Let's hope this is the only one you have."

"A girl can dream," Georgia said with a sigh. She glanced over at Mack. "All finished?"

The officer nodded. "I'll pop by tomorrow if I think of any other questions."

From the way he was looking at her, I suspected Mack would pop by even if he had no questions. Hardy's amused look told me he thought the same thing.

"You ready?" Hardy murmured.

I nodded and covered my mouth to hide a yawn.

"I'll follow you back." He rose and put a hand out to help me up. We said our goodbyes and left, the ambulance tail lights ahead in the distance.

What a day this had been.

TWENTY-ONE

Hardy waited in his cruiser outside the driveway until I made it into the house. I waved goodbye and shut the door, sagging against the frame.

I'd have to go around tomorrow to see if Georgia had found anything else out about the burglar. Plus, I got a battery alert on one of the cameras, so I needed to switch those out.

I realized I'd forgotten to ask Hardy how the escort went, but I was too tired to do anything except kick off my shoes and get ready for bed.

A mental to-do list marched through my brain like a troop of soldiers, keeping me awake far longer than I would have liked, but eventually, I drifted off into a fitful sleep.

The next morning felt like it came way too soon. I blinked awake with a jerk. Light spilled through the window, casting a cheery, warm glow over my bed.

It was beautiful, but I was grumpy. I grunted and rolled over, pulling the blankets over my head.

When it was obvious I wasn't going back to sleep, I blew out a breath and swung my legs off the bed, pushing myself to a seated position.

My slippers waited by my feet. I stared at them for a long moment. The second I put them on, my day would begin.

I glanced longingly at my pillow, sighing at the thought of another long day, but eventually I slid my feet into my slippers and stood.

I was just pouring myself a cup of coffee when someone knocked on my door.

My hand froze in mid-pour. I glared at the door, finished pouring my coffee, then trudged over to it and peered through the peephole.

Mom and Gran stood there looking fresh and cheerful.

I opened the door without a word and trudged back to the kitchen. Mom and Gran stood at the entrance for a moment, exchanged a wordless glance, then came in.

Mom went straight to the fridge and started rooting around. Gran pulled out a flat skillet and a few other things. Before I knew it, both were stirring and pouring, and the smell of melted butter filled the kitchen.

I watched curiously until I realized Mom was making crepes.

One of my favorites from when I was a kid. "I don't have any berries," I said, my voice raspy with sleep.

"It's not a berry kind of morning, I don't think," Mom

said. She handed Gran a container of heavy whipping cream and a bundle of bananas. A jar of Nutella sat on the counter.

"Hazelnut and banana crepes?" I asked hopefully.

Mom winked and turned back to the stove.

Forty-five minutes later, I was stuffed like a turkey. Full of filled crepes and coffee, I felt content and happy.

Gran polished off the last of hers. "Better?" she asked.

I nodded. "Much. I didn't get a lot of sleep last night. Sorry for the grumpy greeting."

Mom laughed. "Not much different from when you were a teenager."

"Mom!"

Gran laughed. "She isn't wrong. You were a bear every time you woke up from the age of fifteen to seventeen. Once you made it to seventeen, we finally started seeing the human aspects of you again."

I rolled my eyes, unable to help the amusement curving my lips. "Lies," I said lightly.

Mom's eyes twinkled. "You know you were," she said lightly. "Now, tell us about why your night was so bad."

I curved my hands around my steaming mug and told them about the break-in at Georgia's shop.

We chatted about that for a while before I slid into the next subject. They were the only two I could confess to about the life changing item I might have who wouldn't judge me or try to take it from me.

"I found something. In the shop."

Mom's brow wrinkled. "Something you didn't already know about? Or did you find something you lost?"

"Nothing like that. They knocked a wall down during the expansion, and there was a massive antique safe in the back."

Gran sat up a little straighter. "Treasure. Tell me it's treasure."

I laughed. "Not quite."

Walking them through it, I told them what I found, showed them online, then told them about Sylvia and the potential upcoming auction. By the time I finished, Mom had sat back in her chair, her eyes wide.

Gran blinked a few times, her mouth open with shock.

They spoke at the same time. "What are you going to do?" Mom asked.

"You can't tell anyone!" Gran blurted.

They looked at each other before laughing. "Gran is right. Tell no one."

"I had to tell Hardy and a few others. Daniel helped me find Sylvia."

Gran sipped her coffee. "I like that young man. He's better suited to your lifestyle."

Mom choked on her tea. "Mom!"

Gran shrugged. "What? He is. If she's going to be a millionaire soon, it will work out even better. That way he knows she's not in it for the money."

I rolled my eyes, even as a laugh bubbled from me. Leave it to Gran to be that blunt. "First of all, we aren't dating and have no plans to."

"Says you," Gran muttered. "That boy looks at you like good butter melting on a hot roll."

Mom murmured something under her breath that sounded suspiciously like, "Heaven help us all."

"We've been friends for a while now. He knows I'm not after his money, regardless." I took one more filled crepe and cut a quarter of it, sliding the small piece onto my plate. I was full, but it wasn't every day Mom and Gran came over and made a fancy breakfast like this, so I'd eat every bit of it and not throw anything away.

"Make sure he isn't after yours if this all comes to fruition," Gran said.

"Even if it does, I'm pretty sure Daniel is set for the rest of his life." I waved my hand. "But we aren't dating, so there's no reason for us to be talking about this!"

Mom gave me a knowing look. "He is handsome," she said slowly.

"There are plenty of handsome men out there, Mom. Plus, I just got out of a serious relationship. I'm not interested in dating anyone right now."

"Well, don't wait too long, honey," Gran chided. "You're young and beautiful and have a lot to offer the world." She reached over and patted my hand. "Now, what do you have to do today?"

I told them a few things on the list, including stopping by Georgia's.

"Mind if we tag along?" Mom asked. "We wiped out all our errands early, and it's a gorgeous day for exploring."

"Sure. Give me half an hour to get ready?"

Mom and Gran nodded. I stood and went to the sink to run some hot water to soak the pan Mom used for the crepes. They both waved me away. "We'll take care of the cleanup."

I smiled gratefully. "I'll take care of feeding you two tonight then."

"It's a date," Mom said.

I forgot that Gran drove like a blind Nascar driver. Mom white-knuckled the handle above her, and I gripped the door handle, holding on for dear life.

Gran cackled like a lunatic every time she took a corner too sharp, which was basically *every* corner. By the time we arrived at Georgia's, I felt like declaring I had a case of the vapors. Gran got out with total nonchalance, like she hadn't just given us both a dozen heart attacks on the drive over.

Mom and I sat in the car for a moment longer before Mom muttered, "That woman is a vehicular menace."

I'd lost the power of speech on the way over, my voice curled in on itself, like it was too scared to come out for fear it would be one long, horrified screech.

When my shaking had calmed down some, I slid out of the car and glared at Gran. She winked and adjusted her massive purse. "Ready to go, slowpokes?"

Mom shut the car door and shook her head. "I'm driving us home," she said, holding her hand out for the keys.

Gran huffed. "Spoilsport," she muttered, but dropped the keys into Mom's palm.

We walked up to Georgia's store. She spotted us right away and waved us in, coming around the desk to greet us.

"Hey, Dakota!" Her gaze fell on Gran and Mom. "I'm Georgia."

"This is my mom, Everly, and grandmother, Charlotte."

"Pleasure," Georgia said. "Dakota has been a huge help to me and the shop. Did she tell you what happened last night?"

Mom nodded. "She always manages to find trouble," she said with a laugh, "but she helps people in the process, so I can't find myself too angry about it."

"Sure seems like it," Georgia said, metaphorically stabbing me in the heart by agreeing with my mother.

She laughed when she noticed my look. "Some people find trouble as easily as others find gold."

"I'm not trying to find anything," I grumbled.

Mom covered up her laugh with a fake cough. I sent her a dark look and set my bag down.

"I got a battery alert, so I came by to change those and check to make sure they're working like they should. Just a precaution after yesterday."

Georgia waved Mom and Gran over to the coffee and tea area. "Go ahead, Dakota, and thank you. I have a few things to tell you when you finish."

I didn't wait to hear what she said to Mom and Gran, instead making my way to the various shelves to pull the cameras down. I found the one that required a new battery and switched it out. Nothing seemed amiss, and once I verified they were all operational via the app, I headed toward the three women.

They laughed at something Gran said, and I smiled as I poured myself a cup of coffee. "All good," I told her. "You should have at least a couple of weeks before I need to check them again."

"Provided no one else breaks into my shop?" she said. There was a haunted look in her eyes. Georgia had a tough week. She'd lost a treasured employee and almost lost her own life when someone came in looking for that book.

"Right," I said. "Did you ever speak to Mack again?"

Her cheeks colored. I suppressed my smile. Those two were definitely going somewhere. "He came by earlier," she said. "Mack said the thief wasn't from Copper Canyon or Silverwood." Georgia shrugged. "He thought the guy might be a day worker traveling around taking handyman jobs for cash."

I frowned. "I wonder how a dayworker would know about the Audubon books. Maybe he's a hobbyist or something?" I didn't want to judge anyone, but these particular books were niche and not well-known by your average reader.

"Easy cash?" Gran interjected. "If he's a dayworker, he probably doesn't care about the book at all. He just wants to sell it for a quick buck."

"Those original texts aren't just a quick buck," Georgia said. "That's retire and disappear kind of money." She shook her head. "I don't know why he thought I might have anything like that. Those are museum quality items."

Georgia snorted and laughed. "If I found those books I wouldn't tell a soul. That kind of money changes people."

Mom and Gran thankfully did not look at me. It *was* that kind of money, and even though I trusted Georgia, I didn't know her. Something like this was the kind of secret you only told your mother. And sometimes not even then.

I was lucky enough to have a particularly awesome mother and grandmother.

"If there is an original floating around, there's probably more than one person involved to help find it," Mom said. "One person doing all that investigative work to track it down to a small area like this doesn't ring true. Normally, it takes multiple people in a situation like this. Someone to find it. Someone to get it. And someone to offload it."

"You think more than two?" I asked.

Mom shrugged. "It's worth millions. Someone taking cash for handyman jobs doesn't seem like the same kind of person who would make collecting rare books a hobby."

"She's right," Gran said. "This girl ... what was her name?"

"Kelsie." Georgia took a sip of her tea. "Though I've come to understand that wasn't actually her real name."

I winced. "Alice Montgomery. She worked for a firm specializing in rare books."

Georgia's hand jerked. "*What?*"

I'd told Georgia about the false identity but had forgotten I never told her what Alice specialized in. "Yes. Sorry. We found out much later. I can only assume she was wrapped up in these thefts."

Georgia's hand shook as she set down her mug. "Well." She smoothed her hands down her pants. "That's unfortunate."

Mom patted Georgia's knee. "People surprise us in the worst ways sometimes. I'm very sorry."

"It doesn't mean she's 100% involved. There could be another explanation for it," I added. But none of us believed it.

Georgia chuckled. "Thanks for trying to make me feel better. But, if she worked in rare books, she made much more money than she ever could here. There'd be no reason for her to come to my shop unless she thought I had the book."

"Unless she was running from something," Mom said, "and the book was a coincidence."

"Awfully big coincidence." Gran shook her head. "It's more likely she was involved than not. I think we look into that before we chalk this all up to coincidence. Because then her death would be an entirely different issue, and that's even more concerning. If the man in custody didn't kill her, then who did?"

Georgia grimaced. "Good point." She rubbed a hand over her eyes. "I guess I need to do a thorough background check for Melissa. She's worked for me a lot longer, but I don't want any more surprises."

I held up a hand. "A friend of mine already did that."

Georgia's eyes widened in surprise. "Who's your friend?"

"Um. I'm not sure he'd like me divulging his access to a system he's probably not supposed to have."

"Fair enough," she said with a laugh. "So Melissa is still good? You haven't found out anything else?"

The hope in her voice broke my heart a little. "All good with her."

She closed her eyes. "Thank goodness."

A thought occurred to me. "Did they get the guy's name who broke in?"

"Oh!" Georgia nodded and dug in her pocket for something. She produced a slip of paper and read from it. "Lars Norton."

Never heard of him. I took out my phone and typed the name into the notes area. "I'll have my friend look into him."

Georgia made air quotes with her fingers. "Tell your 'friend' thank you."

I stood and grabbed my bag. "We won't take up any more of your time. Mom, Gran, ready to go?"

They stood and went to rinse out their cups. Gran took mine as well.

"Your family is lovely," Georgia said, rising as well.

I smiled. "They really are, thank you."

"I'll walk you out." Georgia led us to the front of the store and held the door open as we walked into the chilly morning air. "If I find anything else out, I'll let you know."

"Same," I called, waving at her as we headed back to the car.

Mom nudged Gran out of the way when she tried to

snatch the keys from her fingers. "You are not driving, you old menace," Mom said.

Gran cackled. "You're just jealous it takes you twice as long to get anywhere!"

Mom rolled her eyes. "That's because I like to arrive alive." She jerked a thumb at me. "Get her into the car, please," she muttered.

I laughed and opened the passenger door for Gran. "You heard the sergeant," I whispered.

"Dakota!" Mom barked.

I winced as Grandma chortled.

"See what you did. You got me in trouble!" I mock-whispered to Gran.

"Your mother needs more adventure in her life. This is good for her."

"You still drive like a nutter," Mom grumbled. "That's too much adventure during my golden years."

Gran wrinkled her nose. I ducked my head to hide my smile and slid into the back seat, making sure I buckled up. Mom was right. Gran was a wild woman behind the steering wheel, but Mom drove like a senior citizen with the gas pedal stuck at 20 mph, so neither had much room to talk.

As far as why I didn't step in and drive? Well ... one would have to be a fool to step between Mom and Gran when they wanted to do something. Plus, they made stuffed crepes this morning. I'd endure a little bad driving if I got crepes out of it.

I'd endure a lot of things for crepes.

I spent the rest of the day with Mom and Gran exploring the rest of the town. Much like Silverwood Hollow, Copper Canyon was full of adorable little boutiques, artisan crafts, and handmade jewelry shops. We all came back to the house loaded with goodies, murder and mayhem briefly forgotten.

Mom and Gran plopped onto the couch, kicking their shoes off on the way. I smiled at their antics and went to the kitchen after putting my bags away.

I'd call Cole tomorrow to see if he could tell me anything about Lars Norton. The man was in jail and wouldn't be a bother to either one of us for a while. For tonight, I could enjoy myself and relax with family.

COLE PUSHED a plate of loaded fries toward me. "They're delicious."

I snagged one and popped it in my mouth, chewing as I thought about what I wanted to ask him. I sent him a text last night asking for information about the guy, but Cole hadn't agreed, merely asked me to meet him for lunch tomorrow.

Cole looked relaxed. His hair was a little windblown from sitting outside, the tip of his nose slightly red from the temperature. Green eyes danced from behind his spectacles.

"How's the investigation going?" he asked.

"I have a lot of loose ends and no way to connect them."

"Mind sharing what you got?"

My eyes narrowed, making him laugh. He held his hands up. "Off the record. I only want to help."

"Promise?"

Cole's face sobered. "If I ever say something is off the record, it's off the record."

"I don't have much." I filled him in on what I knew, but most of what I told him was speculation. "The Lars guy is our best bet to figure this out."

Cole winced.

"What?" Tension clenched my guy. "Did something happen?"

"Lars Norton was an alias. Whoever it was escaped police custody early this morning."

I stared at him for a long moment. "Escaped."

Cole nodded. "No one is sure how he got out, but when they went to check his cell, it was empty."

I groaned. "Great. Right back to step one."

"Not necessarily." Cole shook his head. "He wants that book. I don't think he will venture far."

"I still can't figure out how Kelsie got tangled up in this. She worked for Georgia for a while."

"Maybe it started off the right way, and she got tied up in it later. Lars could have approached her and offered her a cut if she helped him get it."

It fit. Even though the woman already worked in rare books, she more than likely only took commissions from sales. Greed motivated people to do many things, and the Audubon work was extremely valuable. "And when she couldn't produce, he killed her?"

"Or she wasn't satisfied with her cut and demanded more money." Cole shrugged. "Could be anything."

"I never met her, so I have no idea what kind of person she was. Georgia didn't seem worried that she was involved in anything shady."

"The closest ones to us can hurt us the most," Cole said. His voice took on a strange note with those words.

I studied him for a moment. "You doing okay?"

A smile flitted over his lips, there and gone in an instant. "Normal stuff. It will blow over."

My heart ached for him. Cole had his fair share of ups and downs lately. He hadn't said much, but I knew he and his current girlfriend were on the rocks. Again. But I didn't bring it up. If he wanted to talk about it, he'd open the conversation. "If it doesn't, I'm here to talk anytime you need."

He reached over and touched my hand. "I know you are. Thank you for that."

We chatted a little more and finished up lunch. Cole promised to check some potential leads out and cautioned me to stay close to home. After we parted ways, I sent a message to Georgia warning her about Lars' escape.

She responded right away, telling me she was closing the bookstore for the next few days. I wanted to tell her it wasn't necessary, but I refrained. If she felt like that's what she needed to do, who was I to stand in her way?

I went back to the shop to check on Harper. To my surprise, Hardy stood at the register chatting with her.

He turned when he saw me, his face brightening. "Ah. Dakota. Just who I came to see."

Harper's brow rose, and she made a circular motion with her index finger, pointing to the back. I nodded, and she slunk away, leaving me and Hardy in the quiet store.

Lunchtime was usually quiet unless it was summer. When it was warmer, we had a steady trickle of browsers.

But today, there weren't that many people in the town square and even fewer browsing customers.

"I heard you lost Lars."

Hardy blinked in surprise before a thunderous frown creased his forehead. "And how exactly did you hear that?"

"A little birdie told me."

He blew out a breath. "He escaped custody early this morning. There was a lapse in—" Hardy paused for a moment. "Procedure," he bit out, saying it like the admission pained him.

"What do you mean by that?"

"Mack and I handed him off to officers at the station. They failed to fingerprint or photograph him, instead putting him in a holding cell."

I stared at him. "Surely someone discovered it later and took a mug shot before releasing him?"

His pregnant pause told me everything I needed to know. I rubbed a hand over my mouth. "Hardy. No one knows what he looks like!"

He turned away. "I'm aware," he growled. "It's bad enough that a potential killer is back on the streets, but what's worse is that those officers who assisted us are gone."

I walked over and sank into one of the chairs. Hardy followed and did the same.

"You think someone posed as a police officer, helped Lars escape, then slipped away?"

"That's exactly what I think," Hardy said. "This is bigger than Georgia's store. Bigger than yours and Harriet's. I did some digging and there have been a rash of bookstore thefts all over the country."

"Rare books?"

"Yes."

I frowned. It didn't make sense. "Can't they just scour the internet and find the sale listings for them?"

"It has to be an underground market."

I snorted. "There's a black market for everything, isn't there?" But I had a book potentially worth nine million, and the thief had stolen many others. Some of the books were too well known to sell outright without raising suspicion. They'd have to keep the sale under the radar.

"It's not book lovers trying to sell these things," Hardy said. "I can only assume the thieves are selling their ill-gotten gains to collectors, the ones who can't obtain certain books by legal means."

"You think it's a network?"

Hardy nodded. "Lars, or whoever he is, is only one man in a group of thieves."

Well, that made this much bigger than anything I'd ever worked on. I suddenly had a very bad feeling. Hardy noticed my expression.

"Dakota?"

I pulled my cell out and texted Daniel.

I trusted him, but I didn't know the people who'd taken the book with them.

My cell phone rang a few seconds later.

"Everything okay?" Daniel said.

"How well do you know Sylvia?"

"Well enough. What's going on?"

"Georgia had a break-in at her shop. The guy escaped police custody with two people posing as officers."

"Okay," he said slowly. "What does that have to do with me? Or Sylvia?"

"Hardy thinks several people might be involved in the thefts. He said there might be an underground market where collectors buy things they can't get their hands on by normal means."

There was a long silence. "You think Sylvia is tangled up in it?"

"I'm not sure. Maybe."

"Well," he said lightly, "she called me and said she wasn't able to auction off the Audubon book for a few more weeks, and she'd like to hold on to it until then. I didn't agree, so I picked it up last night."

An extreme sense of relief filled me. A long, slow breath escaped. "Daniel Jenkins. You are a saint."

"I have a safer spot than anywhere in a warehouse. If Sylvia is involved, she no longer has your book."

A thought occurred to me. "Why didn't she call me?"

Daniel snorted. "She doesn't like you very much."

I gasped. "Daniel!"

"Don't get upset. She's rich and stuck up, and she thinks I have a crush on you."

"Oh." I didn't want to ask, but I felt like I needed to. "You were involved with her?"

He laughed. "You jealous, Dakota?"

I...I didn't know. "Just keep the book safe," I snapped. "And I want a new auction house."

"I figured you'd say that. I already contacted another company. They're supposed to come out tomorrow. I planned to call you this evening. Come for dinner at six? They'll be out at seven."

"I'll be there." Part of me was bummed I had to do this all over again, but at least Daniel had saved the book.

"Dakota?"

"Hmm?"

"He's bringing two potential buyers. There's a strong possibility the book will sell tomorrow."

My heartbeat sped up. "Tomorrow?"

"Yes. Once that wire goes through, you'll never have to worry about another bill in your life."

As good as that sounded, I still had trouble believing I wasn't about to wake up from a dream. "As long as it doesn't get me killed beforehand."

"The book is locked in the vault. Sylvia doesn't know where it is, only that I have it."

"That doesn't make me feel any better. Does she know where you live?"

"She does not, but it probably won't be hard to dig up." I heard the amusement in his voice. "Either way, I don't allow strangers on the grounds without an appointment."

"Just be careful. Thank you so much for doing this."

"It's always my pleasure," he said. "I'll see you tomorrow."

We hung up. Hardy sat a little stiffer in his seat. "You're going to his house for dinner tomorrow?" I wasn't surprised that was the part of the conversation he picked up.

Hardy and Daniel got along like a match and gasoline. "He has a new auction house rep coming over tomorrow, along with a couple of potential buyers. Sylvia wanted to keep the book, but Daniel insisted on picking it up."

"Of course he did," Hardy muttered.

I ignored his snark. "It's possible she's still involved. I'll talk to Daniel more tomorrow."

Hardy stood. "I'll do some digging myself. Any chance of getting an invitation to dinner tomorrow?"

My brows rose. "Why?"

His lips twitched. "For the investigation. And for your safety. If they're looking for that particular book, it's possible they'll show up tomorrow." He patted his hip where his gun lay. "Detective, remember?"

"I'll ask," I grumbled.

He grinned. "Let me know what I should wear," he said before breezing out of the shop.

I sighed and shook my head. Hardy was beginning to be a major thorn in my side. But one positive thing had come out of this. He wasn't so reticent to share details with me anymore.

Harper poked her head out of the office door. "Safe to come out?"

I waved at her. "All good."

She slipped out of the office and went back behind the register. "All good if you need to go."

I shrugged. "There are a few things I need to do before I leave. Anything I need to know?"

"The case hasn't been tampered with that I can tell. I checked the cameras this morning. All good there. The construction crew came in a little earlier than normal, and Mitch didn't say much, so I guess everything is good there, too."

Nothing unexpected. And it was always a relief when Mitch walked in without a clipboard. If he had a clipboard, it meant my pocketbook was about to hurt. If he came in holding a tape measure or a hammer, it was safe.

"I'll check in on things before I leave." Smiling at Harper, I headed back to the office for a little while. I had a shipment coming in from Daniel's publisher in the next day or two and had to figure out where I was going to stock them.

Mitch waved and motioned me over when I walked into the new addition. A few other workers milled around, the tall lanky one bent over a long piece of wood. He held a pencil and a tape measure, carefully marking certain points on the wood.

The place was coming along beautifully, a long line of gorgeous, dark stained shelves lining the back walls. Mitch stood at the new registration desk, a can of matching stain sitting on the unfinished part.

"Wow! You've done a lot since the last time."

Mitch shrugged. "I don't run the kind of business where we stall just to charge you more, Miss Dakota."

I warmed a little more toward the gruff contractor. He'd been nothing but kind to me during the entire time he'd worked inside my shop. "I'm glad to hear you say it, but I already knew that."

We smiled at each other. "What can I do for you today?"

"Just a general check-in. How's it going? Anything I can do?"

Mitch shook his head. "Nothing you can do. I'm a little shorthanded." He sent an irritated glance over at his crew and lowered his voice. "Contractors can be on the unreliable side. Since the work is so up and down, I can't always have the same crew. These guys aren't my usual people, and I can't seem to keep a pin on them."

"Still on schedule for completion?"

"So far," Mitch grumbled. "I might end up working extra hours, but barring any major complications, the completion date is still on schedule."

"I'm flexible. If you need a few more days, we can talk about it."

Mitch waved me away. "Don't need nothing right now." He looked up at me, his eyes twinkling. "But I'll keep that in mind."

The man I'd met before with the contagious smile waved when I passed by on my way to where the safe was. I grinned back and popped my head into the new room. The wooden floor was polished to a high gloss and Mitch had built some shelves on one of the walls. I inhaled the scent of fresh wood and polish, smiling to myself before tapping the side of the freshly painted wall.

Everything was coming together nicely.

I waved goodbye, everyone but the odd contractor waving back.

Maybe he was just a loner and spoke to no one. As long as my new space came together fine, it didn't really matter, did it?

TWENTY-THREE

Daniel took Hardy's invite in stride, murmuring something under his breath before he laughed softly. "Sure. Tell him it's business casual, and to keep his badge and his gun hidden."

"Why does he need to hide his badge?"

"Officers make even the most law-abiding people nervous. These are serious buyers, and if there are people willing to harm them to steal rare books, I don't need Hardy showing up as if he expects that very thing to happen."

"Mmm. Fair enough, I suppose. All right. I'll tell him."

"Good."

I was just about to hang up when Daniel cleared his throat. "Dakota?"

"Yes?" Nerves twisted in my stomach. Why did I think I wouldn't like what he was about to say?

"Look your best." He hesitated. "I know one of the

buyers. He's insufferable. Think about the end goal. It's one dinner that might change your life."

"That sounds ominous."

"Black dress. Black heels. Hair up. Minimal makeup. Can you do that?"

I pulled the phone away from my face and made a face at it. "I can, but I don't want to."

Daniel laughed. "One dinner, Dakota. Just get through it. Once it's over, you'll be able to do whatever you want."

I blew out a frustrated breath. "Fine," I growled. "I'm going to have to go to the store."

"Don't. I'll have something sent."

"Am I in a scene of Pretty Woman?" I muttered.

"This is how the ultra-wealthy live. If you ever wonder why I'm such a hermit, you'll find out in a few hours."

"Should I bring anything?"

"I'll leave something out for you to bring inside. I'll put it in the box right on the porch."

"What? Why? That's really weird."

"It's a bottle of champagne. Take it from the box and bring it inside."

I scoffed. "I can pick up a bottle of champagne."

"It's a thousand-dollar bottle."

"A—what?" I choked on a cough. "A thousand dollars?"

"Welcome to the big leagues," Daniel said. "It's awful here."

"I'll bring it in," I said quietly, empathy for Daniel filling me.

"Thank you." The words dripped with relief.

"I'll see you soon."

We disconnected. I sat at the table for a few minutes longer staring at my cellphone and wondering what I had just walked into.

The doorbell rang at five, but before I could answer it, whoever it was drove away. I opened the door to see a large, rectangular box sealed with a red ribbon.

Okay. I really *was* in Pretty Woman. Shaking my head, I brought the box in and set it on my dining room table. I'd just finished curling my hair and pinning it up into a loose chignon, but I still had to do my makeup.

The dress had made it just in time for me to finish and still have a few minutes left before I had to leave.

The ribbon slid off the box after a slight tug. A slip of black fabric lay in what seemed like a mountain of tissue paper. I moved it aside and pulled out a stunning midi-length dress. There was a box underneath it and a leather roll up. I took both out and moved the box aside. The dress was a stunning satin. It had a modest neckline and thin, sparkling straps, decorated with what I hoped were not real diamonds.

I set that aside and opened the second box to reveal a pair of strappy black heels. Frowning at those, I unrolled the leather pouch.

A pair of diamond earrings and a stunning solitaire diamond necklace lay inside.

"Daniel Jenkins," I murmured. "I hope everything is returnable."

I sent him a quick text.

I hope you kept the receipts.

His wink emoji response did not foster hope.

Sighing, I picked everything up and took it to the bedroom.

It was time to put on a show.

I had just pulled my keys out of my purse when a sleek sports car pulled into the driveway. The dinner started in a little while. No time for company.

Shoving my feet into the surprisingly comfortable heels, I grabbed the small black purse I'd found shoved into the back of my closet and hurried outside, locking the door behind me.

A tall man in a dark suit stepped out of the vehicle. He made no move to come up the steps, remaining by the car.

When he saw I wasn't coming down, he held up a hand. "Daniel Jenkins sent me. My name is Shawn. I'll escort you to dinner this evening."

I sent Daniel a text. He responded immediately.

Get in the car. He's good.

Rolling my eyes, I carefully navigated down the steps, muttering under my breath about the heels Daniel forced me to wear.

Shawn held the door open and waited until I'd adjusted my skirt around me before closing the door.

The seats were slick, black leather, and the car had a deep, luxurious scent. Shawn got into the driver's side without a word and pulled out of the driveway.

"Buckle up, ma'am," he said, stopping at the edge of the driveway.

"Oh! Sorry." I clicked the seatbelt and gave him a chagrined smile.

"No need to apologize." Shawn pulled out onto the road. "Mr. Jenkins said you might be nervous and to do all I can to put you at ease."

I snorted. "This is all Mr. Jenkins' fault.

Shawn's eyes crinkled. "He said you'd say that."

A laugh escaped me. Of course he did. "Do you know anything about the guests?"

Shawn shrugged. "Not much. Mr. Jenkins doesn't go too many places, and I'm only on part-time. One of the buyers is a gentleman named Herman Morris. He's intelligent and well-read. The other is..." His voice trailed off.

"Not very nice?" I questioned.

"I don't find any of them nice," Shawn admitted. "They are different, I suppose. When you have that much money, you don't worry about the same things others do."

I could understand that. Not that I was familiar with being that über rich. Or even a little rich.

"Is the menu good, at least?"

Shawn chuckled. "Mr. Jenkins doesn't often have dinners, but when he does, he ensures he hires the best catering in the entire state."

"At least there's a little good news," I muttered. Then I glanced down at the waistline of my dress and frowned. "Not that there's much room for me to enjoy anything."

Shawn glanced up at me in the mirror. "Don't worry.

He always keeps leftovers. If you're the last to leave, you can take however much you want."

I clapped my hands together. "Something to look forward to."

"If it's the same caterer as last time, make sure you take more than one piece of that divine tuxedo cake."

"You don't have to tell me twice."

We grinned at each other in the rearview.

Daniel's house loomed like a monolith. When I first saw it, I was intimidated, but the man inside the house made the place a home, and not a cold mansion.

Shawn pulled around the drive and stopped right in front of the steps. He put it in park, got out, and jogged around to help me out of the vehicle. I took a few deep inhales and exhales before I took Shawn's hand.

He walked me up to the door, gave me a shallow bow, and lowered his hand to whisper in my ear.

"Good luck, Miss Dakota. Don't forget the champagne." He winked and stepped away, hurrying back down the steps to the vehicle.

A snort escaped me as I watched him. Tonight was already starting out super weird. Let's hope it didn't get any worse.

I reached into the black wooden box. A golden box with a red ribbon lay there, so I scooped it up, replaced the lid, smoothed my skirt, and rang the doorbell.

Here goes nothing.

TWENTY-FOUR

A woman dressed in a maid's outfit met me at the door.

"You must be Dakota Adair," she said.

I nodded and handed her the champagne, but she wouldn't take it.

"Um. No ma'am," she whispered. "You must hand it to the host so everyone can see you do it."

My brows lifted. "Is it always like this?" I whispered.

Her cheeks dimpled prettily as she tried to hide her smile. "Only when Mr. Jenkins is forced to entertain," she whispered.

"How is it in there?"

She shrugged. "Stuffy."

I snickered. "I'm going to be so bad at this," I confessed.

"If I can give you any advice, it's to listen more than you speak. Everyone except for Mr. Jenkins likes to hear themselves talk. They don't like to be challenged."

"Thank you for that," I whispered.

She nodded and motioned for me to follow. I squared my shoulders and let the woman lead me into the thick of it.

Daniel stood in the middle of a small crowd of people. I sucked in a shocked gasp at the sight. I'd never seen him in a tux before, and he looked positively stunning. He'd smoothed his normally unruly hair away from his face, highlighting the sharp angles of his cheekbones. His eyes softened when he spotted me, though the expression on his face didn't waver.

A tall, thin man stood beside him, speaking about something I couldn't quite hear. The other three men occasionally nodded, as if whatever he was saying was extremely important. A woman sat on the couch, dressed in a brilliant blue dress with sparkling silver heels. Her blonde hair was swept away from her stunning face, soft curls spilling down her shoulders.

She had light brown eyes and bronzed skin, and her eyes were not on the conversation.

They were on me.

The woman rose and walked over, extending her hand when she got closer. "Emilie Magron. You must be Dakota."

I shook her hand. "I am."

"Pleasure. I am with Hawk and Martyr."

I blinked. Hawk and Martyr was one of the largest rare book firms in the country.

Her red lips curved into a smile. "I see you're familiar with our work."

"I am. You have the best stock in America. Maybe the world."

"True," she said without a shred of modesty. "Daniel has informed me you are in possession of a great treasure."

"Maybe," I said with a laugh. "I've had it authenticated." My brow furrowed. "Twice actually. The first auction house didn't work out."

Emilie laughed, a low throated sound. "So I heard. It was wise of Daniel to retrieve the volumes. We've heard rumblings of Sylvia's...loyalties."

"I don't know her, but I have heard of several book thefts around the country. Whoever it is seems to be looking for what I have tonight."

Emilie's' eyes lit up. "Ah. A possible hint of danger this evening? How delightful."

My eyes narrowed. "Well, I wouldn't call it delightful. Maybe terrifying. Definitely not delightful."

She flicked a manicured hand at me. "You must not like adventure."

I hadn't been here for five minutes, and I was already exhausted. "I like books, good food, and streaming television."

Emilie's brow furrowed, but I was saved from her reply by Daniel's presence.

He took both my hands. "Dakota." His eyes warmed as he brushed his lips over my cheek. "You look stunning."

"I had a good stylist."

Daniel grinned. "Emilie. I see you've introduced yourself already. If you don't mind, I'd like Dakota to meet everyone else before we talk business."

She inclined her head. "As long as we get to see the volumes soon, you can do whatever you wish."

"All in good time. We have an amazing meal planned before we get to the main event."

Daniel held his elbow out. "May I?"

I slid my fingers over the crook of his arm and allowed him to lead me away. "You owe me so big for this," I hissed.

"The biggest," he agreed. "I'll let you use my library whenever you want."

"I already do."

He took a deep breath and sighed. "True. How about I take you out on the town then?"

I stumbled in surprise. A laugh rumbled in Daniel's chest.

"Like a date?" I hissed.

"Are you asking me out?" Daniel asked.

I glared at him. "I'm not ready to date anyone."

"Then it's not a date. It's a friendly outing."

When I relaxed, he kept talking. "Where I buy you dinner and we go dancing."

"Daniel…"

"We're almost there. Smile, Dakota. Pretend you care about this diner."

"I do care about this dinner," I hissed.

"No," Daniel argued. "You care about the result of this dinner."

It was true. "I'll be on my best behavior."

"You always are," he murmured. "But try not to be too smart tonight. As much as it dazzles me, no one here will appreciate it. They have frail egos and want to be the smartest man in the room."

"I'll do my best to simper and fawn all over every male in this room."

He snorted. "My dear, as much as I would love to see you attempt that, there is someone here who might lose his cool over it."

Hardy Cavanaugh stepped into the room.

He must have already been here because he came from the kitchen area. Hardy was dressed in a dark suit and a satin tie, his dark hair neatly brushed. He held a glass of red wine, and an expression that said he wanted to be anywhere but here.

When he saw me, his eyes brightened. He made a beeline for us, his lips tightening when he saw my fingers curled over Daniel's arm.

"Hardy, this is Dakota Adair."

His forehead wrinkled for a brief second. "So very nice to meet you," he said, reaching for my hand.

"Is this...what is this?" I whispered.

Hardy leaned close. "Daniel gave me a new identity for tonight. I'm Hardy Baxter, rare book collector and trust fund baby." To my surprise, he sounded more amused than angry about it. "I failed to bring my sports car to the party because I am both eccentric and environmentally conscious."

I pressed my lips together to keep from laughing out loud. "Very nice to meet you, Mr. Baxter," I said, loud enough for everyone to hear.

"A pleasure to meet you as well." He winked and straightened.

Daniel watched us, a curious expression on his face. "Would you like to meet everyone, Hardy?" he asked.

"I would." He lowered his voice. "There are plainclothes officers placed at various spots on your property, per our agreement. There's been nothing out of the ordinary yet."

"If anything happens tonight, it will come from inside the house," Daniel said.

My eyebrows rose at the ominous note in his voice, but he winked to soften the edge. Still, the knot in my stomach tightened a little more.

Daniel nodded to the small crowd. "Everyone, please meet Dakota Adair. She's the proprietor of Tattered Pages, an incredible, rare bookstore in downtown Silverwood."

The tall, thinner man from before extended his hand. "Herman Morris. You are stunning, Miss Adair."

Color heated my cheeks. "Thank you, Mr. Morris."

"Herman, please." His hand was cool and dry. This was the man Shawn said was well read and intelligent. He had dark brown eyes and sandy blond hair. Herman wasn't quite handsome, more unique than anything. If I only saw him once, I'd recognize him if I saw him again, no matter how much time had passed.

"Dakota, this is Roy Hanselman."

He was shorter and stockier than Herman. Dark, well-groomed hair, soft blue eyes, and a weak chin. He wasn't quite handsome either. I disliked him on sight, and I couldn't explain why.

And then he spoke.

"Miss Adair. I look forward to seeing this treasure you think you've found."

The barb stung but didn't surprise me. "I've worked in rare books for many years, Mr. Hanselman, but I am not an antiquarian."

Roy's laugh sounded like a braying donkey. "I should say not! You're far too pretty."

Daniel's fingers tightened around my elbow, warning me not to verbally destroy this man.

"Oh!" I pulled away from Daniel and held up the champagne. "I brought this for you."

Daniel's eyes flashed in approval as he took the gift. "So thoughtful!" He peered into the box and clicked his tongue. "Incredible taste, Dakota. I can't wait to enjoy this."

I grinned at his antics. "I thought of you when I bought it."

Daniel's lips twitched. "Then I shall cherish it."

Another man came forward. Taller than the first, with a leaner muscle build, he wore an intense look, though I didn't sense any danger. He smiled and extended his hand. "I am Armand Ferio."

"Pleasure to meet you." I put my hand in his. Instead

of shaking it, Armand tipped my palm over and placed a kiss on the back of my hand. Tingles rushed up my arm.

"The pleasure is all mine." Armand smiled and rose. His skin was sun-kissed, and his eyes crinkled at the edges. He looked like a man who enjoyed life as it came and didn't worry about the future.

"Are you a rare book collector, Mr. Ferio?"

"Armand, please. I am a collector of many things, but I must admit, I am here mostly out of curiosity. Daniel rarely hosts gatherings, and I could not pass up the opportunity to see his wonderful house and the woman he wanted to introduce us to."

Hardy stiffened beside me.

I ignored his reaction. "We've been friends for a while now. We play chess at least once a month." I slid a glance at Daniel. "He's a dirty, lying cheater when it comes to games, but I have yet to figure out how he's doing it."

Armand's eyes widened before he broke into a hearty laugh. Daniel's grin was unrepentant.

"It's not cheating if it's only suspicion," Daniel said mildly.

I patted his arm. "Spoken like a true cheater."

The last man watched the interplay between us, amusement sparkling in his eyes, before stepping forward. "I'm Grant Carlyle, one of Daniel's oldest friends."

"Oh?" I glanced at Daniel.

"Grant doesn't live here," he explained. "He's on a road trip and happened to be close enough to drop by for a little while."

"What state?" I inquired.

Grant frowned. "Montana right now. The winters are absolutely brutal."

Daniel laughed. "Spoken like a true Californian."

Grant's face turned sheepish. "True. If it dips below fifty degrees, I admit I get grumpy about it."

"What do you do in Montana?" I asked.

"I'm in finance and go where the clients request. If they have enough money, I'll travel to them."

I didn't ask any more questions. It sounded like Grant worked with some serious high rollers, as did everyone in this room. Or they were the actual high rollers.

"This is Hardy," Daniel said. "He's a book collector, as well, though he resides in the local area."

Once everyone greeted each other, servers came out with trays, refreshing and replacing everyone's drinks. I took a non-alcoholic cherry spritzer and sipped on it while Daniel and Hardy took over the conversation.

My feet began to ache a short time later, and I was just about to find a place to sit when a bell rang.

"That's the first warning bell for dinner," Daniel announced to everyone, his voice carrying throughout the room. "Shall we make our way to the dining room?"

Relief filled me at the thought of being able to sit down, so I stuck close to Daniel as he led us through the house and into a large dining area. The table was set with stunning China and a gorgeous, fall flower display—so tall diners wouldn't be able to see each other if they sat on opposite sides of the table.

I hadn't sensed anything off yet. This felt like a normal dinner party, albeit one where ten years of my salary would never equal one year of anyone else's here. But as far as murderous intent or theft went, I didn't think anyone here was guilty of it.

I could be wrong, but these people could all buy whatever they needed twenty times over.

Regardless, I didn't plan to let my guard down. Even the most prestigious people could have a dark side.

TWENTY-FIVE

Daniel sat me beside Roy. I sent him a dark look, but Daniel either didn't notice or didn't care. Daniel sat at the head of the table, with Hardy and I on opposite sides in the first seat next to him. Roy sat next to me, and Daniel had put Emilie Magron next to Hardy.

There were far too many forks and spoons and knives, and I stared at them for a long moment, anxiety settling in my gut. I'd have to watch Daniel to see which one I needed for what course.

The bell rang a second time. Two people I hadn't noticed stepped from the shadows and shut the dining room doors. The lights darkened a moment later, lit candles all around the room providing a warm golden glow.

Daniel's foot bumped mine. I glanced up to see him looking at me. He leaned over. "Relax, Dakota," he whispered in my ear. "It's almost over."

The first course came out a moment later, a small salad with figs and goat cheese, dressed with a balsamic glaze.

Conversation lulled while everyone ate. I had to refrain from licking my plate.

Roy kept up a nonstop diatribe of inane dialogue. By the time they cleared the second course, I knew all about the yacht he had on order, his alimony payments to his second ex-wife, and the pending paternity suit he had.

How was a guy like this a book collector? Was it the collection part of it important to him? Or could it actually be the literature?

"So," I said, during a rare lull in his yammering, "are you a fan of Audubon?"

Roy brayed a laugh. "Not at all. I collect things that other people do not have. If this is the real thing, it will go straight into my display room." Roy shrugged. "Where I will show it off during dinner parties." He paused. "And when I have dates." Roy winked. "If something is worth anything, no matter what it is, it impresses the ladies."

I had to physically suppress my eye roll. "Mmm hmm," I said. It was the only thing I could say because how did one respond to something like that?

Daniel bumped my foot again. He knew me better than I thought he did.

"But I doubt it's the real deal." Roy wiggled his eyebrows. "So, I'm just here for the free dinner."

Daniel bumped me again.

"The dinner is amazing." I smiled at Daniel. "Compliments to the chef."

"I'll make sure she knows." Daniel said, tipping his wine glass at me.

"She?" I inquired.

"My cousin," Daniel elaborated. "She'll pop out soon to introduce the main course."

I gaped at him. "Your cousin? How did I not know you had a chef in the family?"

"I guess it never got brought up." Daniel shrugged. "She makes an amazing chicken fried steak."

"I'm going to ask if she knows how you're cheating at chess," I grumbled.

Daniel grinned. "I've never cheated at anything in my life."

A petite woman wearing a white chef's coat came out of the kitchen right as he said it. "Ha!" she crowed. "Daniel is the sorest loser I've ever met. If there's a way to cheat, he knows it!"

The entire table broke into laughter. Daniel's expression turned rueful.

"Thanks for that," he grumbled.

She bent and pecked his cheek. "Hey cuz. You're welcome." She grinned and straightened, waving at us. "I'm Amy Jenkins, chef and cousin to the mysterious Daniel Jenkins."

A few wolf whistles sounded from around the table. Amy laughed and held up her hands.

"The main course is coming up. It's by special request from Daniel and is one of his favorite meals." She went on to tell us about a Sous Vide duck dish with a spicy orange sauce. It sounded weird to me, but I rarely ate anything super fancy. Everything had been delicious so far. My hopes were high.

As soon as the last dish was placed, the dining room doors banged open, startling everyone in the room.

A woman strode in, blonde hair streaming behind her. She wore a teal cocktail dress showcasing dewy bronzed skin. Her green eyes scanned the room, landing on Daniel before a small, satisfied smile curved her lips. Daniel turned toward the interruption and turned white when he saw her.

"Hello, Daniel," the woman purred.

A man came in a few moments later and followed the woman to the next empty seats at the table. The current server got a panicked look on her face and hurried back to the kitchen.

"Mariella," Daniel said. "To what do I owe this pleasure?"

"A dinner party and I'm not invited?" Mariella tsked. "You know how I love parties, Daniel."

"You hit on the keywords. Not invited." Daniel's posture was stiff and unyielding. "This is a business dinner. Not a personal party."

She lifted a perfect shoulder. "You and I must speak. This is the perfect opportunity."

To my surprise, Daniel didn't challenge her. Servers carried out two more plates and set them down in front of her and the unnamed man.

"Who's your friend?" Daniel asked.

"This is Martin Pellman." She flicked her fingers. "He's merely here to ensure my well-being."

I choked on my spritzer. Was she expecting to be murdered?

The quiet conversation around the table halted.

"Are you expecting something violent?" Daniel drawled. "Like you said, this is merely a business dinner."

"I've heard the rumors of what this dinner is about," Mariella said. She smirked, snapping her napkin before setting it on her lap.

Hardy's attention turned to her. He'd been quiet the entire dinner. "Rumors?" he inquired.

She leaned back and studied him. Interest flickered over her face. Mariella moistened her lips. "Well, hello. Who are you?"

I cleared my throat and bumped Daniel's foot with mine.

Daniel tapped the side of my heel with his shoe. "This is Hardy Baxter. He's here for business."

"Ooh. Business," Mariella drawled. "Can't wait."

Daniel shook his head. "You may eat and leave, Mariella. Your presence is not required for a moment longer."

If it were me, I wouldn't have let her eat, but there was something to their relationship that gave me pause.

Ex-fiancée? Ex-girlfriend?

Something else?

I looked down and focused on my duck. Whatever

they were was none of my business. Getting through tonight had to be my first priority.

Ugh. How long could I make this duck last so I didn't have to talk to anyone? Why couldn't we just get down to brass tacks and get these books out of my hair?

I sent Daniel a plaintive look. His lips twitched, but he didn't put me out of my misery. Hardy's face was set in stone. He attacked the duck dish with sharp clicks of the utensil against the plate.

This was miserable.

I leaned closer to Daniel. "How do you do this?"

He snorted. "I hardly ever do *this*."

My heart warmed. He was making himself uncomfortable for me and for the potential this deal had. He'd used all his contacts and spent an exorbitant amount of money to see it through. Tears sprang to my eyes. "Thank you. This is the weirdest dinner party ever, and I appreciate you."

Daniel's eyes crinkled at the edges. He tapped my foot twice under the table. "You're very welcome."

Across, the table, Hardy's knife screeched against his plate.

I locked eyes with him. Anger danced in the light blue depths. Without looking away, I pulled my cell from my bag. Dropping my eyes, I shot him a quick text.

This is not the time.

Hardy looked down. A second later, his lips pressed tight, and his shoulders slumped.

Sorry. You're right.

Would this dinner party ever be over?

TWENTY-SIX

We stood in front of the tall metal door where Daniel kept the volumes. Everyone milled around, Mariella standing inside of Hardy's personal space. Her fingertips rested on his forearm, and she gazed up at him adoringly.

She was a beautiful woman, but every inch of Hardy's body was taut with annoyance. I walked over and nudged him with my elbow.

"What kind of books have you collected lately? I had a Gatsby in the shop, but it sold. First edition."

Hardy extricated himself from Mariella. "It's been a while since I made a purchase. I have a pristine copy of Tom Sawyer, but I bought it several years ago." His eyes sparkled as he looked down at me. "The shop I bought it from is really something."

I suppressed my smile. "Oh? I'll have to check it out."

The metal door groaned as Daniel pushed it open.

"Touch nothing," he warned as he stepped inside.

Hardy held his arm out for me, ignoring Mariella. She glared when I curled my fingers around it. We walked inside, Hardy's steps hitching when he saw the security measures in front of us.

"What does this guy have in here?"

I saw the moment Hardy's eyes landed on the gold. He sucked in a breath. "I'm in the wrong line of work," he muttered under his breath.

I snorted. "You and me both."

Hardy shook his head. "If things go the right way tonight, you might have all of this, too."

"I still don't think it's real." Shaking my head, I tugged Hardy's arm to get closer to Daniel. Emilie was already there, glued to Daniel's side as he unlocked the safe.

"The books or the potential?" Hardy asked quietly.

"The potential more than the books. They've been verified twice. It would be outside the realm of believability for two appraisers to get it so wrong."

"And one of them was your friend," he said. "You've known him a long time?"

"Since college. He's good at his job. Liam wouldn't lie to me."

Just as the lock clicked open, the lights flashed once, twice, three times.

Then the room plunged into absolute darkness.

A shrill scream broke the sudden silence just as a strong, warm arm wrapped around my waist and pulled me against a hard chest.

"Stay with me," Hardy said in my ear.

"They're trying to steal the book." That had to be it. Was this an entire thing a setup? It couldn't be. Daniel wouldn't do that.

"Everyone keep calm," Daniel said. "There's a backup generator. It will click on shortly." The sound of clothing shuffled closer.

"The safe is locked again," Daniel whispered in my ear. "It never opened. The books are safe."

I closed my eyes in relief. "Thank you."

"How long for the generator?" Hardy asked.

The lights flickered before a soft glow illuminated the room.

"Now," Daniel said, his eyes focused on something lying on the floor. His expression was tight and grim.

Hardy swore, loosening his arm from me. He drew his gun.

"Everyone back!" he barked.

Another scream sounded in the room.

"Emilie," Daniel snapped. "Enough!"

"There—there's a body!" Emilie wailed.

"Back up to the wall and sit down," Hardy barked.

When no one moved, Hardy's jaw tightened. "Now!"

The sharp snap of his voice spurned everyone into action. When everyone was sitting on the floor, Hardy pulled his phone out.

"Send assistance to Daniel Jenkin's residence." He rattled off the address. "And a Forensic team."

He spoke a few more commands, then disconnected

the call. "Going out with you is always interesting," Hardy said.

I snorted. "Once again, this is not my fault."

Daniel murmured something to Hardy. His nod was sharp, but he didn't look angry. I gave them both a curious look, but neither would tell me what they were talking about.

Hardy bent down and checked the body's pulse, though we could all tell the victim was deceased based on the small hole in her head and the pool of blood underneath her.

Someone in this room had murdered Mariella.

A chill went down my spine as I realized she'd been standing right next to me before the lights went out.

I took a step closer to Daniel.

"Perhaps I should lock you in one of these safes," Daniel murmured, his eyes locked on Mariella's body.

I touched his hand. "Who was she to you?"

Daniel sighed. "A woman I dated." His lips pressed together. "She wasn't a good person, and I'm ashamed to admit how long it took me to realize that."

"I wonder why she came here tonight?"

"Knowing Mariella, it wasn't anything important. She never liked being left out. More than likely, she just wanted the attention turned on her." He rubbed a hand through his hair, leaving part of it standing up adorably.

I leaned my head against his shoulder. "I'm sorry this happened to her. She didn't deserve it."

His eyes darkened. "No. She was a lot of things, not all of them good, but you're right. She didn't."

The sound of the doorbell interrupted. I jerked in surprise, slapping my hand over my chest to slow my pounding heart.

Daniel winced. "Sorry it's so loud. I always miss hearing the doorbell when I'm in the library. I might have overcompensated."

Hardy rolled his eyes. "Can you grab the door, please?" He still had his gun trained on the rest of Daniel's guests.

"I'll get it," I said, desperate to get out of the room. The doorbell rang again, the sound jarring.

Hardy shook his head. "Not a good idea to go alone."

"Someone has to get it," I argued. "Everyone in the house besides the staff is in this room."

The doorbell rang once again. I sent him a desperate look. "It might be important."

Hardy's jaw tightened. His eyes flicked to Daniel who hadn't looked up from Mariella.

Without waiting for his response, I walked out of the room and hurried to the door.

TWENTY-SEVEN

My heel clicks sounded like gunshots in the quiet house. But something occurred to me as I walked. There were staff still in the house. Why hadn't one of them answered the door?

I took a quick detour toward the kitchen and pushed the swinging door open, poking my head inside.

"Hello?" I called.

Something crashed to the floor—not glass, maybe something metal. I squeaked in fright and backed away, turning to hurry to the door. I'd feel better if the police were in here and not outside.

I used to read far ahead of my grade level, and I think it scarred me for life. After I read a novel about a clown in a sewer while I was in middle school, I had to have a flashlight any time I walked through a dark house. I kept flashlights everywhere when I was younger, much to Mom's chagrin. Now I had little motion lights all over the house.

They put off a warm, friendly glow that put off just enough light for me to make sure no bogeymen were hiding in the corners while I hurried to my bedroom to go to sleep.

This run to the front door kind of felt like that now. The house was lit well, but unfamiliar and every shadow made my heart pound in my chest.

Plus, this house was enormous, and it felt like it took an hour for me to get where I needed.

I skidded to a stop and peered through the peephole. Two paramedics and three uniformed officers stood there.

"Thank goodness," I breathed right before I opened the door.

The paramedics asked a few brief questions before rolling a stretcher through the door. I directed them to the back while the officers followed. They knew I was here with Hardy, so they didn't ask any questions as we walked.

I waited outside the door while they worked, eventually taking a seat against the wall. The officers were busy questioning all the guests, and Hardy was with Daniel speaking quietly in the corner. When he glanced at me, I motioned for him to come over.

He held up a finger for me to wait a minute, so I leaned against the wall and waited, making sure I had a view of the room and the hallway. There was still no sign of the kitchen staff.

Hardy came over a few minutes later. "Everything okay?"

I told him about the kitchen. His brow furrowed as he glanced at Daniel. "They probably have a separate way out. Though they shouldn't have known what happened here."

I hadn't thought about that. Hardy got Daniel's attention.

"Where are your kitchen staff?" he asked.

Daniel blinked. "If they finished cleaning up, they have quarters in the basement."

"And the person who answered the door?" I asked.

"She's probably home by now." Daniel stared at us like we were nuts. "What's going on?"

Hardy still had his gun out, lowered but still ready. "How well do you know your kitchen staff?"

Daniel stared at Hardy for a long moment. "My cousin brought them. I'm sure she knows them, but you'll have to ask her." His expression fell. "Have you seen Amy?"

I shook my head. "A bowl or something fell in the kitchen when I checked, but I couldn't see anyone."

"We should go look for her," I suggested.

Hardy's look was withering. If we were in different circumstances, I might have laughed. Instead, I jerked my head toward the kitchen.

"If it wasn't any of them, then it might have been someone in the kitchen. We need to make sure Amy is okay, as well as any others caught up in this mess."

He holstered his gun and jogged over to the other officers. They conferred for a minute before Hardy came back over and took me by the elbow.

"Can't promise anything," he said to Daniel. "But if your cousin is out there, we will find her."

Daniel dipped his head. "Thank you."

"Come on," Hardy said to me. When we were out of earshot, he spoke again. "You are maddening," he muttered. "If danger was a whirlpool in the middle of the ocean, you'd steer right toward it."

I tugged my arm out of his grip. "You make it sound like incidents like this are a thrill I can't get enough of."

"Aren't they?" he asked, his eyes looking ahead for danger.

"What?" I asked, bristling with outrage. "Absolutely not! What I'm not willing to do, though, is leave someone at the mercy of a criminal because something is dangerous. And neither should you! Especially not you!"

Hardy blew out a frustrated breath. "A woman was shot in a room we were all standing in, and you think someone in the kitchen is guilty?"

"You think I'm a silly ninny, don't you?"

Hardy stilled, finally looking down at me. "Nothing of the sort."

"We should find her and help her because it's the right thing to do," I said quietly. "Not because you think I'm running into danger just for the thrill of it. I'd much rather be in my pajamas, having a glass of wine, and mindlessly watching a show. Wearing a fancy dress and heels is torture."

Hardy's throat worked. "You think it's torture to wear them?" he murmured. "It's torture for me to see you in them."

I blinked, color flooding my cheeks when I realized

what he meant by it. "Hardy," I hissed. "This is not the time."

He chuckled under his breath. "You might not like it, but I could stare at you for days and never get tired. Even when you wear sweats and a tank, Dakota. You're always beautiful to me."

I shook my head. "Come on," I croaked, pulling him forward. "We can talk about this later."

"Will we?" But he let me tug him closer to the kitchen.

I ignored him and stopped at the door, waiting for him to go ahead. He reached for his gun, put me behind him, and headed inside. I crept behind him, wondering why he hadn't made me stay in the room with Daniel.

As gruff as he could be, and as much as he hurt my feelings sometimes, he was learning. He wasn't trying to force me under his thumb. Here I was walking into danger with him.

It felt weird, but I was appreciative that he trusted me enough to follow him into this.

"Stay behind me and stay quiet," he whispered. "If I tell you to run, I need you to listen."

"Okay," I whispered back.

"I'm serious. I can't lose you."

The quaver in the last sentence gave me pause. I came closer and tucked my fingers through his belt loop. "I promise."

Hardy stopped and peered around a corner before leading me out. "There's the bowl." He pointed up at a teetering pile of metal and plastic bowls. "I'm not sure it was anything other than poorly stacked. Could be just a coincidence."

But he didn't put the gun away.

He walked the entire kitchen, then led me downstairs. There was a hallway of six rooms, three on each side. I knocked on the first door and breathed a sigh of relief when a woman answered. Hardy stepped in and asked a few questions, but she hadn't seen anything and seemed really confused about why we were there.

We did the same for the other five rooms, but the story was all the same. No one had seen anything, which was good news.

Except for the second part.

No one had seen Amy since dinner ended.

TWENTY-EIGHT

Daniel sent me a text as we trudged back upstairs.

She's not answering her phone or her texts.

Worry twisted in my stomach. I sent him a reassuring text back letting him know we were looking for her and that the kitchen staff were all safe and under strict instructions not to open their door unless it was him or Hardy knocking.

I'm going to have a tough time hiring kitchen staff after this was the dry text he sent back.

Daniel had a small guesthouse at the back of the property. He'd shown it to me during the tour he'd taken me on but told me it was rarely used. This was the first place I thought of, and I told Hardy as much.

"The team is still in place outside. No one has seen a thing so whoever this was had to be on the premises already."

"You still think it was one of the people with us?" I

asked. The outside was lit but long shadows gave everything a creepy, sinister look.

"I don't know what to think." Hardy huffed a laugh. "Murders aren't usually big mysteries," he admitted. "Most of them get solved within a day or two. Someone got angry. Someone knew the victim. Someone did something they can't take back. It usually is that simple. But I find when you get involved in things, nothing is ever simple."

"Uh. Thanks?"

Hardy chuckled. "It wasn't a compliment, but I will say I've become a better detective since you've been around."

I stared at his back. "I'm not sure how to take that one either."

"That one is definitely a compliment."

Hardy's eyes scanned the horizon, his gun lowered but ready. "This place is something else," he mused. "How much property does he have?"

"No idea," I admitted. "Acres and acres, I assume."

We were about to step out of the backyard into a more wooded area. He held his index finger up to his lips. "Listen for anything suspicious. Breathing, cracking branches, anything that doesn't sound right."

"All right," I breathed.

"Stay close."

We stepped farther onto the property.

Hardy moved like a ghost. I was more of a wounded wildebeest caught in a fishing net. Finally, he stopped and turned. "I hear something up ahead. I want you to stay here. I need the element of surprise."

It didn't hurt my feelings because every time I took a step and heard how noisy I was, I cringed. "Alright," I whispered.

"Don't come out unless I call for you."

I nodded. "Be careful."

His teeth flashed white in the darkness. "I'm always careful."

His flippant words settled something inside of me, but I still reached out and gripped his hand. "I'm serious, Hardy."

He squeezed back. "I will."

Hardy slipped away like a wraith while I leaned against a sturdy tree and watched him.

The sound of raised voices came through the noiseless night. I couldn't make out what they were saying even while straining to listen.

It sounded like a man and a woman. No one should be back here this far onto Daniel's property without permission. Since he said no one used that guesthouse, I could only assume it was either the murderer or Amy had hurried out here. But from the way the voices rose, I had to assume it was both of them.

I hoped Hardy could diffuse it without getting hurt.

Several minutes passed. I was getting antsy about staying where I was and not knowing if Hardy was okay.

A gunshot rang out into the night.

I sucked in a gasp of fright and stepped away from the

tree. My first instinct was to run, but there was no way I'd leave him here.

I wouldn't leave Amy either.

A hoarse shout cracked through the night just as a shadow shot through the woods. Tall, thin and probably male, but that was the only thing I could make out. Whoever it was ran in a strange lope, grasping the side of their waist.

I pressed back against the tree and watched. The person wore a mask and all black and was heading straight for me. My heart raced like a rabbit's, and I stepped around to the other side of the tree and waited.

I had no weapon or anything to defend myself with, but the person was wounded. If he spotted me and tried to attack, I probably had a good chance of getting away if I fought back.

But it didn't answer the question about Hardy. Where was he? And was he okay?

Was he the one who fired the gun? From the way the person was running, I could only assume Hardy had done it. There had only been one shot.

They loped closer and closer.

"Dakota!" came a shout from several feet behind the running person. It was Hardy. "Get back to the house!"

I glanced back toward Daniel's mansion and, remembering my promise, was about to make a run for it, but I saw Hardy running toward me, a limp body in his arms.

A chill ran down my spine. Instead of running, I steeled myself and waited for the perfect moment.

When the person got close enough, I stepped out and extended my leg.

The resultant trip took us both down. My back hit the ground, forcing the breath out of my lungs in a painful whoosh. Based on the pained shout from the other runner, I pegged him as a male.

And potentially seriously hurt by the loud cracking sound when he went down.

Hardy came up on us a moment later, gently laying his burden down. He gave me a long look before pulling handcuffs from behind his back and snapping them on the prone man. He searched him, paused at the man's back, and tucked something in his jacket pocket. When he was finished, he came back and helped me up.

"I saw a chance and took it," I blurted.

A muscle in Hardy's jaw ticked. "I know. And we got him." He gently squeezed my shoulder and pulled his cell out.

He walked off and barked some words into the speaker.

The person Hardy was carrying stirred. I hurried over and crouched, breathing a sigh of relief when I realized it was Amy. She seemed mostly unhurt, though she winced when her eyes blinked open.

"Where's Daniel?" she asked.

"Don't worry. He's inside the house."

Her eyes fluttered shut. "Thank goodness."

I brushed her bangs away from her forehead, wincing when I saw the lump rapidly forming a black and blue bruise. If it looked this bad in the dark, it was going to look a lot worse tomorrow.

"You should see the other guy," she croaked.

I helped her sit up. "You mean that guy?" I asked, pointing to the man glaring at us from a few feet away.

Amy blinked in surprise before smiling. "He got him?"

"Sure did."

"Good." She touched the bump on her head and winced. "I hired him on as kitchen staff for Daniel's dinner, and everything was fine until I saw him sneaking out and following you."

I was going to crow about this to Hardy. So it *was* one of the kitchen staff!

"I called him back, and he acted like he was confused, but when everyone left and I was heading to the guest-house to spend the night, that joker followed me and cracked me in the head right when I stepped onto the porch to empty the dust pan!"

Hardy made it back. "You saw him following us?"

"Yeah. And he was holding something in his hand. I couldn't see what it was, but the whole thing was weird, you know?"

"Very weird." He didn't tell her what happened with Marielle, but he did pull something out from his jacket.

A gun with a silencer on the end. I froze.

"Did it look like this?" he asked.

Amy's eyes went huge. Her throat worked as she tried to swallow. "Err. Yes. I didn't realize it was a gun. All I saw was the long part at the end, and the lighting wasn't so great."

"Don't worry about him. We're going to bring him to the station as soon as the others get here. Paramedics are coming to check you out. We'll wait for them to get here before we leave." Hardy tucked the gun back into his jacket and helped me up.

Flashlights appeared in the distance. Hardy shouted and waved his hands above his head. The light found us a second later.

Police and paramedics swarmed. Hardy steadied me with a hand on my shoulder. "I'll get you out of here in a few minutes, Dakota. Hang in there."

I sighed and leaned against him. Hardy stilled in surprise, then wrapped a hand around my waist and pressed his face into my hair, breathing deep.

Just because you broke up didn't mean you stopped loving someone.

Love wasn't a faucet. You couldn't turn it on and off whenever you wanted.

You could stuff a rag in the hole and slow it down, but eventually, it would all come rushing out again.

TWENTY-NINE

Daniel rushed past us on the way to his cousin, stopping and blurting out a message before hurrying away.

I blinked. "I have no idea what he said."

Hardy laughed. "Something about a check and a text."

Frowning, I shook my head. "No idea."

"We can text him later. Need a ride home?"

"Don't you have to stay?"

Red and blue lights flashed over Daniel's house. Multiple police cars and two ambulances waited in the front circle of his drive.

What a night.

"No. A supervisor came onto the scene a little while ago. He has my initial findings. I'm supposed to be off duty tonight, so he let me go." He winced. "It might be a long day tomorrow, but I'm off the hook for tonight."

"What about all the other guests?"

"Free to go now that we got the other guy."

Speaking of the other guy, two police officers walked past us, each holding onto the arm of the guy who'd killed Marielle.

I was a little disappointed to realize I'd never seen him before.

Hardy stared at the guy until they'd shoved him into the back of the police car.

"Amy got lucky," I observed.

"She fought back and gave me enough time to get there. But I agree." He shook his head. "But something is bothering me about that."

I tilted my head up to study him. "What's that?"

"He had a gun. Why didn't he kill her?"

Fear walked cold fingers down my spine. "I think he wasn't meant to kill Marielle."

Hardy's jaw tightened. "That's what I'm afraid of."

He led me to his car and opened the door. "I think you should have Harper run the store for the next day or two."

"I need to hire another helper. Harper's been a good sport, but it's not fair to her when I need more time off."

Hardy grinned. "You might have all the money you need to hire anyone you want soon."

I rolled my eyes. "After that debacle? I've no doubt I'm shunned in high society."

Hardy laughed and shut the door.

The drive home was done in a companionable silence. Hardy looked as rumpled and tired as I did.

"Those books are becoming the bane to my existence," I grumbled when the car stopped in the driveway.

Hardy grinned before sliding out of the driver's seat and jogging over to open my door.

"You going to try to sell them one more time?"

I barked a laugh. "I'm going to let things marinate for a while. Not because I'm scared of another hit attempt."

Hardy's eyebrow rose. "You aren't?"

"I'm more scared of having to wear high heels again," I said with a groan.

He walked me up to the door and took my keys to open the door. Once I was inside, he reached in and tucked an errant strand of my hair behind my ear. "Call me if you need anything."

"I will. Thanks for having our back tonight, Hardy."

"I always have your back. Lock up tight and stay out of trouble. The guy we got is not the same person who attacked Georgia, so be very careful over the next few days. We're going to work on that guy to see who he's working with, but it might take a while before we know anything."

"I'll do my best."

He shook his head, amusement flashing in his eyes. "Keep your location on."

I gave him a silly little salute and shut the door. I didn't plan for my location to move for at least the next twelve hours.

THIRTY

Poppy had a vet appointment later that week with a new doctor close to Copper Canyon. I planned to stop by Georgia's and make sure she was doing okay. She wasn't great at answering her texts in a timely manner these days, so I wanted to see her with my own eyes.

Poppy hated traveling in the carrier, but I couldn't take her inside the vet without it, so I popped it in the car but let her sit in the passenger seat on the way to Georgia's.

The less time she was inside the carrier, the better mood she'd be in when we made it to the vet.

Poppy hopped up into her little net hammock thing I attached to the window and promptly rolled onto her back where she wiggled into a comfortable position and fell asleep.

Oh, to be a cat.

Chuckling to myself, I made the short drive to Copper Canyon, singing along to the radio as I drove.

When Poppy yowled her displeasure as my voice cracked during a high note, I laughed out loud.

She cracked an eye open and gave me a disapproving look.

"Oh hush. You live a life of luxury. The least you can do is put up with my bad singing every once in a while."

Poppy huffed and plopped her head down right as I turned into a parking spot.

I wasn't sure how Georgia would react to a cat in her bookstore, so I left Poppy in the car and poked my head in to greet her.

Georgia's eyes widened in surprise. "Dakota. Hi!" She smiled and waved me in.

"My cat is in the car. Mind if she comes in for a minute or do you want me to leave her inside?"

"A cat?" Her smile widened. "Yes, yes, yes! Bring her in!"

I held up a finger and hurried back to the car where I scooped Poppy into my arms and plopped a kiss on top of her head. "This is Georgia's store. Be nice to her and her books. You hear me?"

Poppy meowed which I took as a good sign.

Georgia held the door open for me. I stepped inside with Poppy still in my arms, her ears twitching as she checked everything out.

Georgia gasped when she saw her. "So pretty! Such a beautiful orange. May I pet her?"

"Of course. She'll let you know if she doesn't want you to."

But Poppy merely stared at her with those chartreuse eyes and submitted to Georgia's ministrations.

As soon as she stopped, Poppy squirmed and hopped out of my arms.

I glanced at Georgia, but she didn't seem to mind. "Let her explore. Customers will be charmed by her."

"As long as you don't mind."

I sat and visited with her for about twenty minutes, with no sign of Poppy the entire time. When I checked the time, I jerked in surprise. If we didn't leave soon, we'd be late for our appointment. Thanking Georgia, I washed my glass out and went looking for Poppy, finally finding her in the same area I'd found Kelsie.

She sat on the carpet right where her body was found and meowed at me, pawing the area where she'd lain.

When I bent down to scoop her up, Poppy scooted away and bent her head to the carpet, something I'd rarely seen her do. She sniffed, jerked her head back, moved a few inches over, then did the same thing.

I waited for her to finish. Whatever she was doing, I didn't think she'd stop until she was ready.

"We're going to be late," I chided.

Poppy took one more circle around the spot before coming up to twirl between my ankles. I scooped her up and hurried to the car, waving at Georgia on the way out.

This time I stuck her in the carrier, much to her extreme displeasure.

Poppy glared at me the entire ride back home from the vet's office.

"I know. How dare they give you a life-saving shot?"

She meowed in agreement to my sarcasm. Laughing, I turned into the bookstore parking lot just to check in with Harper before heading back home.

Poppy hopped out of the car and waited by the shop door. Harper spotted her before I got up the stairs and opened the door for her.

"Hey Dakota! I'm surprised to see you today."

"Just wanted to pop by and make sure everything's okay."

"All good. The bird book is still in the case, so whoever it is seems to know it isn't the valuable one."

"Worth a try." I shrugged, dropping my purse onto the counter. "How's construction?"

My phone rang. Hardy's name popped up on the screen, but I pressed the button to send it to voicemail. I'd call him back when I was in the car.

Harper shrugged. "Mitch and a couple of his guys got here early, but I haven't heard a peep."

Poppy headed into the construction area. I called her back, but she ignored me. Rolling my eyes, I followed her. "Let me grab her real quick," I said.

Harper waved me away.

My cell rang again. Hardy again. Frowning, I pressed the voicemail button one more time. Weird. Poppy stopped and studied Mitch, giving him a little sniff and twirl around the ankle before dismissing him.

Mitch's befuddled look made me laugh. "Don't mind her. She's just checking you out."

Poppy did the same thing with the the one with the great smile. She gave him a couple extra twirls when the man exclaimed something in a different language and gave her a couple of scratches behind the ear.

My cell rang again. What in the world? I checked the screen to see it was Hardy. Again.

Poppy went over to the last workman, the tall thin one who never spoke to me. She stopped abruptly, her tail rising in the air.

Odd.

I answered the cell.

"Dakota!" Hardy barked.

"Yes. What's going on? Everything okay?"

"The third person, the one who said his name was Lars. Do you remember him?"

"I do. Why?"

Poppy didn't twirl between the man's ankles. She sat and stared up at him with an unblinking stare. I started to get a weird feeling in my stomach.

"Where are you?" His voice sounded near panicked.

"At the shop. I brought Poppy to the vet earlier and stopped in to talk to Harper before going home."

"Listen to me. Get Poppy and Harper and get out of the store."

"Oh?" I kept my voice breezy. "Why's that?"

Poppy bared her teeth and hissed. The frowned down at her before his eyes slid my way.

"His partner has been posing as a workman to get work at bookstores so they could search for the Audubon book. I'm on my way to you. If you can't get out, try to stall."

"Huh. Well, I'll be. What a coincidence." I bent down and called Poppy to me. "Come on now. We gotta get home."

Poppy turned and stared, her green eyes blinking slowly before she turned back to the .

"Hang on a sec. I have a message coming in. It might be important. I've been waiting all week for a shipping update."

"Dakota! Wait!"

I pulled my phone from my ear and pulled up my messages, finding Harper toward the top. I typed out a quick message.

Get out of the store. Right now. Take nothing.

I put the phone back to my ear. "All taken care of. Sorry about that."

"You're out?"

"Harper is taking care of it."

The bell over the door rang, sending a flooding sense of relief over me. All I could do was pray it was Harper leaving and not a customer coming in.

"You're with him. Aren't you?"

"Sure am. I'm catching up with Mitch about the progress."

Hardy swore.

Mitch straightened, his gaze flicking from me to the, then down to Poppy.

"Dakota? Everything okay?"

I shot him a reassuring smile. "Everything is great. I gotta get home. Call me if you need anything?"

Mitch nodded, his brow furrowing. Smart man.

"Poppy. Come on." I took a few steps closer, sending a smile to the . "She just got some shots at the vet. Sorry she's a little grumpy."

I scooped her up and backed away. "I'll call you on the way home, okay?" I said to Hardy.

"No. Stay on the phone."

"All right. You be careful too." I hung up the phone.

But the had caught on. He held a gun in his hand, pointed at me and Poppy.

"You aren't going anywhere," he growled.

THIRTY-ONE

Harper had made it out. Lars, or whoever he was, took my cellphone, but text messages were going off every few seconds.

"Where is it?" he growled. "I know you have it. It was in that safe, wasn't it?"

I sat, tied up, in an uncomfortable wooden chair from the construction area. "Where's what?" I asked, pretending to be clueless.

"You know what I'm talking about. You tried to sell it last night!" He didn't look so harmless now. The man was still tall and painfully thin, but his eyes burned with a dangerous zeal.

"That was a dinner party for a famous author." I shrugged. "He wanted to show off his collection of rare guns."

Daniel had zero guns, but this guy seemed like he liked them, so maybe I could distract him with that for a while.

The sound of sirens came in the distance.

Lars' attention snapped to the window. "You called the police?"

I shook my head. "You have my phone."

"It's that man, isn't it! The one in here all the time."

I saw no point in lying. "Yes. He's on his way. If you leave now, you'll have time to get away."

"I'm not leaving without that book," he snapped.

Stalling for time wouldn't work for long. "It's not with me. It hasn't been since the day I found it."

Triumph lit his eyes. "So you do have it!"

"I did. Not anymore."

Mitch sat in another chair a few feet away, his face a mask of fury as he watched his workman. "I ran a background check on this guy, Dakota. I swear."

A laugh bubbled from my throat at the ridiculousness of our situation. "I'm not mad at you."

"Shut up!" Lars barked. "Where is the book now? And hurry."

The sirens grew closer.

"It's in a locked vault."

His eyes flickered. "At that author's house?" Lars grinned. "Not anymore. My guy must have it."

I didn't tell him his guy was locked up and about to serve at least twenty years in prison. He pulled his cellphone out and dialed a number, frowning when no one answered.

"Where is he?" he snarled.

White flashed in my peripheral vision. I didn't dare look in its direction.

"Who?" I asked politely.

Lars looked like he was about to have a coronary event. He came closer, looming over me. My heart pounded against my rib cage, blood roaring through my veins. I'd get out of this. I had to. Poppy had jumped out of my arms as soon as Lars pulled the gun. I hadn't seen her since, and all I could hope was she was either hiding or had somehow made it out of the store.

"My partner."

"I left the party early. It was uneventful, and no one there was interesting, so I caught a ride back home after dinner."

He had no way to know since his contact was sitting in lockup.

The heater kicked on with a click. Lars jerked, his attention snapping above us. I chanced a glance over and saw Hardy at the window. He was making a circle motion with his fingers. I had no idea what it meant, so I frowned. Lars shifted, and I tore my eyes away from Hardy's.

The shop phone rang. Lars cursed under his breath. "Where is it?" he growled. I pointed behind the counter.

He hurried over and picked up the phone before slamming it down. A second later, it rang again. I bit down on my smile at the enraged look on Lar's face. It had to be Hardy calling the line to distract Lars from whatever they were doing.

Mitch carefully scooted his chair back to where his

foot was at the edge of a tall bookshelf. He looked at me, down at his foot, then back at me. When he did it again, I watched as he lifted his foot and pressed it against the bookshelf's base.

When I realized what he planned, I winced but nodded. Damaged books were never good, but our lives would always be more valuable. The difficult part would be getting Lars to stand in the right place to make it work.

Mitch cleared his throat. "I'll be docking your pay, you understand?"

Lars spun, his mouth open in shock.

"Mitch," I hissed. There was no reason to antagonize a man waving a gun around. He had to get Lars closer, but I could have thought of a million other things to do it other than what he chose.

But Mitch had chosen violence today, and Lars responded.

He stalked up to Mitch and leaned close to hiss in his face. "Once I have that book, you'll never see me again." His face creased in a manic smile.

Something clicked from behind us. Lars' head snapped up. He started to rise, but Mitch leaned back and shoved with all his might.

Several things happened at once.

Books tumbled from their shelving as the bookcase teetered precariously.

I pushed myself backward in the chair, as far away from it as I could get, landing painfully on my right shoulder. The bookshelf tipped, sending books flying everywhere.

Lars shouted in alarm but couldn't get away from it before it tumbled down, trapping him underneath.

Hardy and two officers rushed in, Harper behind them, her eyes wide and frightened.

"Dakota!"

I waved my hand like a white flag, white stars bursting behind my eyes at the ache in my shoulder.

Hardy cursed and skidded toward me on his knees. "Don't move." He touched my shoulder with tender fingers. A burst of agony tore from my throat.

Hardy winced. "Chuck! Call the paramedics."

"Got it, boss," said a blond man, concerned brown eyes staring down at me as he said something into his radio.

"Is it broken?" I croaked.

"I think so," Hardy said. "Collarbone, maybe. I'm not a doctor." He plopped down beside me and carefully cut my bindings away.

I lay there for a second and breathed through the pain.

"You're going to be the death of me," he whispered.

I closed my eyes and let the darkness claim me.

I stared at the computer screen and blinked, then lifted both hands, rubbed my eyes, and looked again.

"What did you do?" I said to Daniel Jenkins who sat across from me in my shop cheating at chess again.

"I didn't do anything," he said, far too much innocence in his tone. "You solved a crime while also finding one of the most valuable and coveted literary treasures in history. Every single one of my male friends is smitten with you, by the way," Daniel added, a growl in his voice as he said it.

I laughed. "What's a little murder at a dinner party?"

The numbers flashing in the unfamiliar account on the computer screen was enough to give me a heart attack.

"Is this...real?"

"Yup. The books are being shipped to the buyer somewhere to Europe as we speak. Incredible find, Dakota." He sat back and studied me. "What will you do now?"

"Uh. Wait to ensure this doesn't disintegrate into thin air?"

Daniel's eyes crinkled. "I oversaw the transaction myself." He straightened. "Oh. Before I forget." His fingers fumbled through his pocket before pulling out an envelope. "Here's all the account information. I'm on it as a joint owner for now, so we will need to take care of that tomorrow."

Tears sprang to my eyes. This money was life changing. I could retire and never work again. I could...I could do anything.

I rested a hand over my racing heart. "This is too much. I can't think about it right now."

"You don't have to. Close the browser window, take a deep breath, and lose a few more games to me."

I snorted. "As long as you pour me another glass of wine."

Daniel grinned. "I'll pour you two, Dakota. You deserve it after everything."

"Yeah," I agreed. Lars, who turned out to be a man named Christian, confessed to Kelsie's, aka Alice's murder, after she tried to blackmail him into sharing more than they agreed. Just as Cole and I suspected.

Hardy was up to his ears in casework, but he and I had formed a tentative truce, and dare I say, we were on our way to a genuine friendship. Different from the last one.

It felt deeper somehow. Stronger.

I liked it.

The shop door opened, and Hardy walked in, holding

a bag from my favorite restaurant and a bottle of wine. He waved the keys I never took back from him. "Hope you don't mind."

Daniel looked up in surprise and back at me, his brow furrowing in curiosity.

"Let's take a quick break and eat," I said. "Then Hardy is going to watch us play chess so he can finally figure out how you're cheating me."

Daniel's jaw dropped before he burst out laughing.

It warmed my heart when he motioned for Hardy to take the chair next to him.

Friends.

A strange circle to be sure, but it was enough.

Maybe in the future Hardy and I could have more again, but if it wasn't meant to be, I'd settle for a friendship as long as he stayed in my life. Maybe there could even be something with Daniel, but for now, I was content to build this odd house and watch it settle onto the landscape. I had too many questions and not enough answers in my life, but for once, I felt strangely okay with it.

ALSO BY S.E. BABIN

A Shelf Indulgence Cozy Mystery Series

How about a ghost whisperer in a new magical town? Check out The Psychic Cleaner series!

Psychic Cleaner

Like a little more magic with your cozies? Check out The Magical Soapmaker Mysteries!

The Magical Soapmaker Mysteries

If you'd like a little more action and sass and don't mind some PG-13 language, check out my Aphrodite series.

The Goddess Chronicles

Or, if you like a snarky bartender with a secretive mixed heritage, meet Violet!

Cocktails in Hell

ABOUT THE AUTHOR

Sheryl likes cake too much and can be found hoarding it while hiding from her children in the pantry closet.

Follow her on Amazon at: https://www.amazon.com/S-E-Babin/e/B00J1J236A